Hope and Destiny

Koby Crisp

Copyright © 2023 by Koby Crisp

All rights reserved.

No portion of this book may be reproduced in any form without written permission from the publisher or author, except as permitted by U.S. copyright law.

Contents

1. Chapter 1 — 1
2. Chapter 2 — 5
3. Chapter 3 — 10
4. Chapter 4 — 14
5. Chapter 5 — 18
6. Chapter 6 — 21
7. Chapter 7 — 25
8. Chapter 8 — 28
9. Chapter 9 — 34
10. Chapter 10 — 38
11. Chapter 11 — 42
12. Chapter 12 — 46
13. Chapter 13 — 50
14. Chapter 14 — 53
15. Chapter 15 — 59
16. Chapter 16 — 63

17. Chapter 17   67

18. Chapter 18   72

19. Chapter 19   76

20. Chapter 20   79

21. Chapter 21   83

22. Chapter 22   88

23. Chapter 23   93

24. Chapter 24   98

25. Chapter 25   101

26. Chapter 26   105

27. Chapter 27   108

28. Chapter 28   111

29. Chapter 29   116

30. Chapter 30   119

31. Chapter 31   125

32. Chapter 32   129

33. Chapter 33   135

34. Chapter 34   140

35. Epilogue   143

Chapter 1

Rain pounded relentlessly as Hope made her way through the empty streets, shivering as the cold droplets struck her skin and ran in rivulets down her face, masking the tears that she couldn't stop despite her best efforts. Not a soul stopped to ask her if she was alright, and the few cars that were still around at this hour drove past without stopping. More than once she had to dodge to get splashed as one careless driver or another drove through the deep puddles, though it wouldn't have mattered - she was soaked to the skin, and felt as if she were soaked under her skin as well.

Her feet were sore by the time she reached the bridge going over the river, and there she stopped, looking down on the rain-speckled dark water. The river was running much higher than usual thanks to the recent heavy rains, and as she leaned on the railing, Hope wondered how long it would take her to drown. Watching the turbulent waters swirl by, she judged it wouldn't take too long. Death seemed to welcome her with open arms, and in a swift movement, she kicked her shoes off. One fell into the river, quickly disappearing under the turgid water, and the other she left lying where it fell. Let people guess what had happened to her, she thought, as she climbed carefully over the railing. Looking down again, she shuddered, doubt seizing her mind as she balanced on the narrow bit of concrete that stood between her and death. Her body still ached from the beating her father had given her after discovering the positive pregnancy test she'd neglected to throw out, and his words of disgust still rang in her ears, hours later. He'd not been best pleased to find out she was pregnant, but that had come less from an outraged father's perspective, and more from a jealous lover's.

Hope shuddered. James had always been wildly inappropriate with her, and with no mother in the picture, he'd gotten away with a hell of a lot. As a child, Hope hadn't found his overtly sexual advances too disturbing, thinking that was how all dads showed love to their daughters. It was only when she'd gone to the doctor's for a routine checkup that the sexual abuse had been discovered, and all hell had broken loose after that. Hope had been placed in foster care for a while, but James had won her back by claiming it had all been made up, forcing Hope to lie to the authorities on pain of severe beating, if not outright death.

Thereafter, James' advances had become a lot more covert, and now that Hope had been outed as a liar, any claims were dismissed as more lies, thanks to the small-town mentality where everyone's business was known by everyone else. Hope had had no chance of getting the help she so desperately needed, and now, being pregnant, things were going to get a lot worse. She now bitterly regretted the impulse that had led to the one-night-stand, and as she stood on the narrow ledge, mentally steeling herself for the jump that would end her life, she reflected that, by killing herself, an innocent life would be spared from the horrors that surely would be inflicted on him or her.

A car honked, loudly, snapping Hope out of her reverie, and she half-twisted, groaning when she recognise the red Escort. James would never let her go, and he proved it now as he got out of the car, scowling at his daughter as the rain plastered his thinning brown hair to his face. "The fuck you think you're doing?" he demanded. "I didn't give you permission to kill yourself. You're mine, remember? And that brat of yours is mine as well. Get the hell over that railing and in the car, or so help me God, I'll fuckin' strangle you to within an inch of your life!"

"You kicked me out," Hope said, thankful her voice was steady. "You said you never wanted to lay eyes on me again. Well, I'm doing what you wanted."

James lunged at her and grabbed her arm, twisting it painfully and causing Hope to cry out. "You're mine,

" he repeated. "So get the fuck over the railing before I--!"

He got no further; Hope swung wildly, her free hand connected with his nose. He swore and let her go, but that proved her undoing as she lost her balance, and she screamed as she fell, bracing herself for the hard smack as she hit the water. It hurt more than she expected, knocking the air from her lungs as she sank like a stone, her scream becoming a gurgle as the murky water closed over her head. Flailing, lungs bursting, she kicked, twisting about desperately, trying to find the surface. But it was too dark for her to get her bearings, and her heart hammered loudly in her ears as she flailed about, bubbles filling her vision. Already darkness was creeping in the corners of her already obscured vision, and with a gurling sob, she let go, relieved at the end that she'd managed to get free of her father before he could inflict any further harm on her or her unborn child.

Chapter 2

Hope's eyes fluttered open, and for a moment, she wondered if she was going mad - that she'd died and this was the afterlife. Fairy lights greeted her returning vision, and, as her spinning senses adjusted, she realised for the first time tonight that she was warm and dry. It made for a shocking contrast to her soaked state earlier in the night, and she relaxed, sensing that she was also safe for the first time since fleeing her house earlier in the evening. She was still wary, but for the moment, she knew she could trust whoever the owner of this house was.

Apart from the fairy lights adorning the canopied bed in which she lay, the room was unlit, save for a lamp on the bedside table, shaped like a unicorn, glowing brightly in the darkness. It reminded hope of the gorgeous unicorn night-light her mother had given her for her fifth birthday, but James had smashed it not long after his wife passed away, telling the terrified five-year-old Hope that she was too old to be using nightlights. Thereafter, she'd been forced to sleep in the dark, and her screams of terror had only brought smacks across the face.

But while her heart ached for the loss of the pretty nightlight, Hope found comfort in this very similar styled lamp that kept the darkness at bay. Even now, she was still scared to go to sleep in the dark, and she was grateful to the house's owner for thinking of her comfort. Outside, the rain was still pounding down like all the furies of heaven, but she was safe, warm and dry. Comforted by the knowledge no further harm would come to her tonight, she closed her eyes and allowed herself to slip back into sleep, confident her road would be smoother after this.

She woke the next morning with a raging hunger, as well as a desperate need to visit the loo. Outside, the sky was grey, with the threat of more rain on the way. But Hope wasn't worried; she was in a nice, dry house, and the carpet, when she set her bare feet on the floor, was wonderfully luxurious to a girl used to bare floors and thin rugs that did nothing to warm the feet on chilly mornings. A deep plum colour, it was dotted here and there with spots of yellow, green and white, giving the illusion of a flower-covered forest floor, and it was as soft as anything Hope had ever set her feet on.

To her relief, a door to one side led into a bathroom, and once she'd done her ablutions. she felt much better. Reaching for the white fluffy dressing gown on the back of her bedroom door, she let her mind wander to just what would be expected of her in return for the immeasurable kindness she'd been shown. She had not a penny in her name, and she wasn't very good at domestic tasks, her father never having taught her. But she knew she'd be able to negotiate something, and this made her feel better as she all but tiptoed to the stairs, hanging tightly to the banister as she made her careful way down. Her near-drowning of the night before had left her badly shaken, and when she pushed open the dining room door, from which the most amazing smells wafted, her heart lifted at the sight of the gorgeous breakfast spread laid out on the table. That was when she noticed there were some women in the room, and she flushed as she let the door swing to behind her. "Sorry," she said meekly. "I didn't know there was anyone else here."

"Don't fret thyself," one of the women said, her accent proclaiming her a Yorkshirewoman. "Tha's had enough trouble to give thee a right scare; get some vittles in thyself. There's more and enough for everyone."

"Thank you," Hope said, feeling much more at ease. In no time at all she had a plate made up, and soon she was digging into the most delicious breakfast she'd ever had in her life. True, it was two slices of toast, a side of bacon, and a poached egg, but, having grown up on old, mostly out-of-date porridge, the toast, bacon and egg felt like a feast, as did the orange juice which followed. A maid in dark brown, with a crisp white apron, appeared when Hope's plate was cleared, and she took the dirty dishes away, causing the girl to blush again. She almost got to her feet to offer to help, but decided against it, knowing she'd be more of a hinderance than a help.

"Feeling better?" the Yorkshirewoman asked kindly.

"Yes," Hope admitted, a genuine smile on her face for what felt like the first time in forever. "But if you don't mind my asking, where are we?"

"We're in a nice cottage in Helmsley," the Yorkshirewoman said. "Right agin the North York Moors." Her tone was one of fondness as she said this. "It's quite a pretty little place, you have to admit."

Hope's eyes were wide. "I've never been to the North York Moors," she admitted. "Mum always wanted to take me there - she's from Yorkshire - but Dad didn't want to let us out of his sight."

"Ah." The Yorkshirewoman nodded. "Men can be right sods - well, 99% of them anyway. And there go me manners. My name is Emma, and I feel a right naff for bein' so rude to thee."

Hope had to smile again. "I'm Hope," she introduced herself, giving Emma's hand a firm shake. Penny, Daisy and Mia, who were also from Yorkshire, joined in the introductions. "You're going to love it here," Mia told her. "It's quiet, out of the way, and the only thing expected of you is to just be happy and let your cares go."

"I can try," Hope admitted, dread resurfacing despite the good energy coming from her new friends. "But I'm worried about my dad."

"Thy dad is not going to darken thy doorstep," Emma said firmly, a compassionate light in her eyes. "'E were picked up by the local boys in blue last night, and 'E's facin' some charges that'll ensure 'E won't be seein' the light of day anytime soon. And," Emma added, "no one can come here without Eldon's say so. He's got some strong energy protecting us, and anyone coming here with ill intentions won't find nowt but empty moors and some sheep, if they're lucky."

A tingle ran over Hope's body - not of fear, but of curiosity. "I'm sorry," she said. "Did you say ... energy?"

"Magic, good luck charms," the like," Mia said. "Either way, it's pretty powerful, and Eldon is the best around at protecting people from harm. You'll meet him later, but right now, all you need to do is relax and get your strength back. Questions and answers can come later."

Reassured, Hope let her curiosity go for the time being. It was enough that she was safe - the future had no power for the moment, and even should this Eldon fellow turn out to be a charlatan, he had to be better than the brute who called himself her father.

Anyone had to be better, Hope added quietly to herself.

Chapter 3

Over the course of that first day, Hope soon learned everyone on the farm was expected to do chores. She was surprised to find out she didn't mind this at all, even if she was woefully hopeless. But no one upbraided her, or called her stupid, instead taking the time to teach her how to clean, wash dishes, milk cows, and so on. Living in suburbia all her life, Hope was a little overwhelmed at the serene country lifestyle she was now living, but she adjusted to it readily enough, and before long, she felt as if she were a true country girl.

All the women on the farm - ranging from sixteen to sixty - had simliar stories to Hope, and as the days passed, she learned they'd all come to the farm seeking something different, and had been told by Eldon about life on Pandora, and how soon his ship would come and take them away to start a new life. He hadn't told them why he was seeking women, but since his ownership of the farm wasn't too onerous, and he didn't seem the type to demand they hand over all their worldly goods in payment, none of the women minded one little bit. It was enough to know they had a roof over their heads, food in their stomachs, and shelter from the outside world that had treated them so cruelly.

Hope herself wasn't awfully worried about what the future would bring, though she remained skeptical about the mysterious Eldon's intentions. So far he hadn't made an appearance, and when a week had passed, Hope began to have serious doubts that he even existed. All the women swore up and down that he did, but he often left the farm to go to his supposed homeworld, for reasons even they didn't know. He would never anwser anyone's questions as to what awaited them on Pandora - if the place even existed! - and while most of Hope's new companions weren't worried, she was, very much so. If he existed, he was a likely a cult leader, and his "recruitment" was clearly nothing more than a veil to conceal the nefarious intentions she was sure were lurking in his heart. Why else gather vulnerable women and have them work on a farm in the middle of nowhere, isolated from the rest of the world by so-called "protections"?

But, despite her doubts, Hope found herself enjoying her life on the farm immensely. Even if she ended up being shipped off to some Middle-eastern country to become part of a ruler's harem, she reasoned it had to be better than what awaited her back in Oxford - and she wasn't keen on being stuck in her father's clutches once again.

Two more weeks passed, and at the start of the fourth week, Eldon returned. Hope didn't know what she was expecting, but she hadn't bargained on how ... ordinary the man looked. He wasn't unattractive, with dark brown hair, hazel eyes, and a stocky strength underneath his wiry frame. He looked more like a banker, or an accountant, than a resident from another world, and Hope found some of her ever-present doubts ease when he greeted her that afternoon. "So you're the latest stray," he said, shaking her hand with a warmth that put her even more at ease. "Well, you're not the first rescue we've fished out of a river in the middle of the night, and I'm sure you won't be the last. What's your name, love?"

"Hope," she replied, smiling at the wicked humour in his voice. "It's very nice to meet you." She didn't want to say she was sorry for doubting he was real, but he caught her unspoken words and grinned.

"I know," he said, looking chagrined. "I do apologise for not being here to greet you personally - there's a lot of politics involved in this venture of mine, and the heads at home want to be sure this is a worthwhile investment.

I think it is, but they're the ones who have the final say so."

"What do you mean?" Hope asked, confused.

Eldon took her hand. "I'm planning on saying something to everyone," he told her, leading her into the dining room, where the rest of the community had gathered upon learning of Eldon's arrival. "I've managed to get the heads at home to agree - in principle - to my scheme. They're the ones who'll say yay or nay when you arrive in Pandora, but even if they say nay, none of you will be forced to return to Earth."

Hope frowned, more intrigued than anything, and as she found a seat next to Mia, she wondered if perhaps the story of Pandora was actually true? Eldon was certainly spinning a slick story, but Hope thought to herself that maybe, just maybe, there was a grain of truth in there somewhere. But there was only one way to find out for certain.

Chapter 4

"**I**'m going to be as blunt as I know how," Eldon told the assembled women, his easy humour gone, to be replaced by a stark gravity that stunned them all. "Pandora is dying."

Dead silence greeted this, and he smiled thinly. "I don't mean it's dying," he amended, "but the population is. You see, we have almost no women, and with no women, there's no children, or grandchildren, and so on. A dreadful disease has either killed or rendered almost every woman infertile, and we're in a crisis such as we've never seen before.

"So we need help, desperately. We tried contacting the native races who live on Pandora, but they've one and all said no - not because they don't like us, but because they don't want the risk of this disease impacting their numbers as well. We've therefore had to resort to very desperate measures. And that's where you lovely ladies come in. In short, we need women, badly. Not for the sole purpose of babymaking, I can assure you, but that is the end goal, and the one reason why the council agreed to my crackbrained idea. And you aren't the first group of women who've gone to Pandora to try and help repopulate the place. Sadly, they either died or became infertile as well, and all the babies who survived carry the gene for the disease, for what reason we don't know. But it left us in an even worse position, and the council was very wary when I told them to make this an official venture, so we could have the proper checks and balances in place to ensure any fallout could be contained. But I promised to take the fall if things couldn't be contained, so the council have agreed, in principle, to making this an official venture, rather than the experiment it was prior to this.

"You'll therefore notice that I've included some women who are already pregnant. Your babies will be born - hopefully - without the disease carrying gene, and we can use them as a building block to start eradicating the gene by virtue of the fact they were conceived here on Earth. As for those not pregnant, I'm certain your babies will likely be as, well, clean as the babies already in their mothers' wombs."

He took a deep breath. "I know it sounds crass," he said, "and now that I've got it in the open, I feel dirty, if you want the unvarnished truth. So if any of you choose not to take part in this venture, I won't hold it against you, and you'll be free to go about Pandora to your heart's content - and there is no legal or moral obligation for you to take part in any case. As I said, the baby making isn't the be all and end all, but it is one of the main reasons I gathered you here in the first place.

But the council are reasonable, as am I, and when we land on Pandora, you'll be given time to settle into life there, and no demands will be placed on you until you come to either the council or myself to say whether or not you'll take part. All of you will be treated very generously and kindly, and you'll have the run of the planet no matter what path you choose to take."

"What is the disease?" Mia ventured, breaking the shocked silence once Eldon had finished speaking.

"It's the Earth equivalent of cancer," Eldon replied, his tone curt. He softened his harsh words with a lopsided smile. "Sorry. It's a very sore subject, but I'll tell you this much - your worst and most aggressive form of cancer here on Earth is a common cold in comparison to what the disease does on Pandora."

Seeing that it was indeed a sore subject for him, Hope framed her question carefully. "When do we leave?"

"In a few days," Eldon said, giving her a grateful smile that thanked her for her tact. "I've just got to tie up some loose ends, but we'll be ready to leave a week from now. I'll leave you ladies to it, but don't hesitate to come to me if you have any concerns." He managed another lopsided smile. "Even if it is about our... ah, I'll call it cancer for lack of a better word. You'd mangle your tongue if you tried to say the Pandoran word for it."

Hope admired his bravery as the meeting broke up, but her mind was buzzing with a million new questions, and as she made her way back to the fields, she felt her newfound ease frizzle away into fresh uncertainty. She shoved the feeling down; if Eldon was telling the truth, she had a new and exciting life to look forward to, and for the first time since finding out she was pregnant, she found herself looking forward to her baby's birth. If newborn babies were going to be the basis of the Pandoran population's survival, she wanted her unborn child to be a part of it.

Chapter 5

Hope's doubts were reawakened rather sharply when, the following week. Eldon roused the little community at the break of dawn. Once everyone had packed what meagre belongings they had, Eldon then led them into town, from where, he said, they'd catch a bus to York station, and then on to Kings Cross. They'd then board the Eurostar to France, and this raised more than one set of eyebrows, Hope's included. Emma summarised the feelings of the group during their walk. "Has tha lost thy mind?" she demanded of the man who had promised so much, and yet, to date, had delivered so little.

"No, tha hasn't lost his mind," Eldon replied, mimicking Emma's accent so flawlessly the Yorkshirewoman had to give him a grudging smile. "I know it sounds crazy," he added, returning to his normal accent. "But trust me, this is the best and easiest way to get to Pandora. Earth and Pandora lie very close to one another in the solar system, but Pandora is actually a half-step out of time with Earth. However, the closeness of the two worlds enables very swift travel, and the Eurostar to France is the point where the barrier between worlds is the thinnest. Specifically, the Channel Tunnel is the entry point between the worlds. When we reach that point, I'll transfer us onto the corresponding train, and that will deliver us safely and easily to Pandora. The journey through space is the more conventional way, but there are risks to unborn children that I won't sanction. And the best part of our route is that we can get to Pandora with a lot less fanfare than if we'd gone the traditional way."

Hope sighed. "You really have lost your mind," she muttered. Her hopes and dreams of an escape from her abusive father were melting away faster than the snowman James had forced her to watch melt as a child, and she felt the same sick feeling now as she did then, but the sensation was much, much more acute.

Eldon, to his credit, didn't try to reassure them further, instead letting silence reign as the bus arrived. Hope blessed him for his tact, even as she resented him for being such a damned charlatan. Idly, she wondered what she'd do when the Eurostar delivered them to Paris, but the sick feeling spoilt her daydreams, and as the bus carried them to York station, she gave up and stared moodily out of the window, wishing no one had come and fished her out of the river that night.

The train ride to Kings Cross was very silent and strained, and the walk over to the Eurostar platforms was equally tense with a pulsating resentment that grew by the moment. None of the women were quite prepared to give up on Eldon just yet, but the sentiment was clear - when they reached Paris, as surely they must, Eldon would be handed over to the authorities as a fraud and a charlatan. The man himself said nothing, not in commiseration or condemnation, but Hope could sense the calm radiating off him, and she wondered, as they boarded their train, how the hell he could sleep at night. He hadn't told them anything about Pandora, and when Emma raised the question as the train got underway, he said soothingly that Pandora was a place that had to be seen to be believed, and that words would not do it justice.

Hope rolled her eyes. "Jerk," she muttered, before giving it all up as a lost cause and resigning herself to the new fate of becoming a rich man's mistress on the other side of the Channel. That seemed the more likely option, and she could tell by the strained faces around her that her friends were feeling exactly the same.

On the plus side, it meant getting away from her father, and even if she did become another man's concubine, it would have to be better than the fate James surely had in store for her once he got out of jail.

That's not my problem, she told herself, but try though she might to look on the bright side, the tears of disappointment rolled down her cheeks for a very long time.

Chapter 6

H ope wasn't the only one who gasped when, 35 minutes later, the train emerged, not in France, but in a world which seemed to come out of a fairy tale, and her eyes widened when she saw the planets in the sky. One had rings, like Saturn, but the other was huge, both dominating the deep blue sky, shining almost as brightly as the moon on Earth. But it was clear this was not Earth, and Hope mentally apologised to Eldon for all the names she'd called him during their jouney from London to … well, Pandora!

"Bloody hell," Mia whispered, and Hope echoed her sentiment as the train made its way through the valley towards a shining city in the distance. It, like the two planets in the sky, shone brightly, like a beacon of hopes and dreams, and Hope felt her heart lift, her eyes filling with tears of wonder.

"This is home," Eldon said, letting the amazing city do the talking for him. "And that's the capital - Isonor."

As the train drew closer, the city grew larger, until it filled the sky, and by the time the train pulled into the spacious station, Hope's doubts had finally melted away - especially after seeing the sky when the train had first emerged from the tunnel. Pandora was real, and it was gloriously, almost frighteningly so.

The station itself was breathtakingly gorgeous, and as Eldon led them through the grand concourse, Hope took in all the sights, smells and sounds. It looked very much like Earth at first glance, but as the group made their way past the inhabitants, there were many subtle differences to clue the Earth women in that this was not Earth. The humans, for example, looked very much like people on Earth, but there were subtle differences, such as the faint golden skin, and the cat-like eyes, coming in a wide variety of colours, as did the hair, making some of the Pandoran humans look as if they'd just stepped out of a rainbow factory gone mad. Their manner of dress also varied - some Pandorans wore styles that wouldn't be amiss on Earth, while others wore elaborately styled clothing that wouldn't have looked out of place in a fairy tale. And there were others who wore almost next to nothing, causing some of the older women to mutter. Hope was no prude, but even she admitted that some of the clothes - or lack thereof! - were a bit on the risque side.

Eldon glanced over his shoulder as he led the group out to the street, where even more wonders awaited them. "Don't judge," he advised. "You're as alien to them as they are to you - don't start off on the wrong foot. They've as much right to what they wear - or don't wear - as the next person."

His rebuking tone quelled the mutters, but as the women got into the pearl-white bus which waited for them, Hope got the feeling that things had already started off on the wrong foot. She herself wasn't bothered too much, but she sensed the older women were not going to adjust to life here quite as easily. Aoife, one of the oldest women, looked like she wanted to tear strips off some of the more scantily-clad men and women, and since she was a devout Catholic, her morals were going to be outrageously upset. "Hey, let's not make waves," she advised the Irishwoman. "We're probably on thin enough ice as it is - I for one don't want to see us kicked out before we've had time to get settled into the place."

Aoife huffed and folded her arms. "I don't have to like it," she said crossly. "Have you seen what some of those huss--"

" Stop," Eldon ordered, his good mood gone as he glared at the Irishwoman. For the first time, Hope saw that his pupils were now slitted like a cat's, and she wondered when he'd shed his disguise. That was soon cancelled out by worry as the Pandoran man continued his upbraiding. "You're all here on my good word," he told them, his stern words and glare encompassing them all. "If any of the council see a reason to have the lot of you kicked off, they'll seize it. I told you this is not set in stone - I have yet to introduce you to them, and right now, I don't feel like painting any of you in a good light, given the atrocious behaviour I'm seeing."

"Hey," Mia protested. "Don't lump us all--" It was her turn to be cut off as Eldon directed his glare at her.

"All of you are on notice," he said, any traces of the easy-going manner he'd first shown them gone. This was the real Eldon, and Hope suddenly realised she didn't like him one bit. But she held her tongue as he continued. "I don't want to hear anything further concerning my people," he said. "Nothing good, nothing bad. And for that matter, since we're on the subject, from now on, none of you are to speak unless spoken to, not even to each other. Do I make myself clear?"

There was a general grumbling assent, and Eldon nodded, satisfied. "Good," he said, but as he turned back towards the front of the bus, Hope had the feeling his ears were pricked like a cat's, and that even the softest whisper would reach him. The other women seemed to sense it; not even daring to mouth words to one another, in case he heard the movement of their lips, they subsided into a sullen silence that pusled with resentment. Hope didn't blame them one bit; she felt the same way, and once again, she wished she'd never been rescued. Drowning, she thought sullenly, would be preferable to this horrible feeling of helplessness.

Chapter 7

Eldon's mansion, located on the outskirts of the city, was an enormous, sprawling affair, and as they made their way inside, Hope couldn't help but admire the place. Her good mood was soured, however, by the fact she couldn't comment on the opulence, and her delight soon turned dour again. The other women all looked as sour as she, but, forbidden to speak as they were, they couldn't express their frustrations. The best they could do was roll their eyes at one another, though they were very careful to make sure they did this when Eldon's back was turned.

The inside of the mansion was just as gorgeous as the outside, but it was the staff who caught Hope's eye. All of them, man and woman alike, seemed to be made out of pure silver, with glowing, electric blue eyes that gave the impression of stripping one's skin until one's soul was bared to the light of day, with nowhere to hide. But it was the fact all of the silver people were naked as the day they were born which caught Hope's attention. Her eyes widened, and she could almost hear Aoife's silent fits behind her, but none of the women said a word, not wanting to be dressed down again. The silver people, in any case, didn't pay the Earth women any more mind than they might have paid to insects, and Hope felt sick all over again.

Eldon led them upstairs, and when they came to the first floor, a gorgeously appointed corridor, he turned to them. "At least you've all got the good manners to keep your mouths shut," he said, his voice cold. "Though I don't appreciate the eye-rolling; I thought you were all somewhat mature, and not schoolgirls in the bodies of women. Never mind; you can roll your eyes all you want. Just bear in mind that your future is still very much up in the air. My staff have their orders; you will not speak to anyone unless spoken to, even when you're in the same space together. That goes for conversing with one another; my staff have eyes everywhere.

What you do in the privacy of your own rooms is your business, and you can yap to the walls all you want. Yes, Aoife, that includes you," he added, with a dire glare directed at the Irishwoman. Aoife looked like she wanted to melt into the ground, but Eldon spared her no pity. "This floor of the house has been given over to your use for the time being," he said, the implication being their continued presence would be contingent on their good behaviour. "All your meals will be delivered at set times, and you're free to roam this floor to your hearts' content. But remember; when you're not in your rooms, you're not to say a word to anyone unless you are addressed directly. Do I make myself clear?"

Once more, the women grumbled assent, and Eldon nodded, before snapping his fingers. Twenty staff appeared as if by magic. "You'll be escorted to your rooms now," he told the women. "I have to go see the council to let them know you've been delivered safely, but if any of you think you're off the hook..." He tapped his temple. "I have a direct neural link to all my staff. I'll be able to home in on the culprit if I should hear anything untoward, and I will come down on all of you like a ton of bricks. I hope I don't have to break off my meeting and come here to have your ungrateful backsides dropped back in the United Kingdom, because I will be very angry if all this comes to naught." Having delivered this final salvo, he stalked off, and Hope swallowed as the staff approached the silent group of women. One by one, they wer led away, and Hope let out a soft sigh once the door of her room had closed behind her. She didn't hear the snicking of a key in the lock, but when she tried the handle, it wouldn't budge, and her heart sank as she dropped to the floor, letting her head rest against the wall. This was worse than being under her father's roof, and she closed her eyes, deciding the best plan, for now, was to do nothing, praying that Eldon was simply suffering from stressed nerves. The alternative - that this was the real Eldon they were all now seeing - did not bear thinking about.

Chapter 8

After lunch - which was surprisingly similar to what one might find on Earth - the women were let out of their rooms, and told they had the afternoon to do as they pleased. Unlike Eldon, they were more civil, which eased the towering resentment somewhat, but there was still a boiling sense of frustration at not being able to vent their feelings to one another, and as Hope went in search of entertainment, the feeling of isolation grew worse, until she felt she could bear it no longer. Her stress, in part, was eased when she found an enclosed swimming pool, and in short order, she changed into a swimsuit she'd found in her wardrobe. The water was warm on her skin, easing some of the tension in her body, and once she'd gotten used to the water, she took a deep breath and went under, shutting the world out and leaving her resentment and hurt on the surface.

For a little while she let herself float just under the surface, exhaling slowly, until lack of air forced her above water. But she didn't stay long on the surface, going under again once she'd got her breath back, letting the water cradle her, trying to forget all she'd discovered in the last few hours, wishing there was someone, anyone she could talk to so she could vent her worries about this new place. She wasn't going to call it home - it didn't feel like home, but there was, she knew, nothing waiting for her back on Earth, except for her father, desperate for vengeance. As she came up for air again, she made up her mind that, should the chance arise, she'd remind the other women they'd come here to get away from life on Earth, and that the same old miseries would waiting for them. She could only hope, as she went under again, that she'd actually get the chance, and that the others would listen, and not let their foolishness get in the way of the new lives they hoped to lead. They were, Hope reminded herself, guests on another world. They had no right to criticise Pandorans for wearing what they wore, or didn't wear, in some cases. They had to abide by the local rules now, and if that meant swallowing their outrage and venting in private, well, Hope knew she was prepared to bite her tongue until it bled, if it meant staying here. She didn't want to go home and face her father, because he'd kill her before letting her escape again, and that was not something she was keen on, not for her, nor for her unborn child. For both their sakes, she prayed she'd have a chance to get her friends to see the light.

Later that afternoon, the staff collected the women and led them back to their rooms, where they'd wait until dinner time. Nothing was said on how the meeting with the council was going, but none of the women were allowed to ask in any case, and the staff didn't volunteer any details. Hope amused herself by sitting at the window and watching the shining city below her, and when dinner arrived, she ate with gusto, feeling better now that she, at least, had come to a resolution to hopefully get her friends to see the light.

No chance was given that night, however, nor the next day, and it wasn't until the morning of their third day in the city that Eldon finally reappeared. His face was like stone as he gathered the women in the ground floor study, and Hope felt her heart sink to the soles of her feet as she found a spot on the couch. Eldon didn't look like the same urbane man who'd spoken so compellingly on Earth, and Hope once more had the nasty feeling this was the real Eldon. She kept her mouth shut, however, resisting the urge to shiver as his hazel eyes swept over them all, no trace of his former warmth showing. "Well, I am not entirely impressed," he opened. "I understand there is a ... handful of you who are not good at obeying orders."

Hope felt shame scorch her from head to toe, but that feeling soon passed when she saw that Eldon was glaring at Aoife, Emma, and Daisy, much to Hope's dismay. Emma had been the first friend she'd made when she'd woken in the Yorkshire cottage after her rescue, and Daisy had also been the soul of kindness to her. To know Emma and Daisy were just as rigid as Aoife was a nasty shock, and Hope shook her head as the three women sat in silence, their faces showing their shame.

I wondered how long it would take for Aoife to break the rules, she thought dully.

That tears it, then. Dad's going to be furious when he gets his hands on me again, if he doesn't just slit my throat and dump me in the river to make sure it sticks this time!

Eldon spoke again, cutting through Hope's dismal monologue. "I knew Aoife was the ringleader," he said, "but I thought better of you and Daisy. Who did it?"

Emma spoke slowly, reluctantly. "Aoife came to me first," she muttered, staring at the floor. "She told me 'twasn't right for women to wear almost nothin' but the skins they came in. I tried tellin' her to shut her gob, but she rode right over me, tellin' me I was a sinner, and that there'd be no chance of redemption unless I saw her way of thinkin'."

"Emma came to me in tears," Daisy confessed. "She told me she'd come to see the light, and that it was her job to save the rest of us." She met Hope's eyes, her own eyes filling with tears of shame. "She wanted me to go to thee," she said, fighting sobs. "I'm so sorry; Aoife and Emma were determined to save us all, especially the young girls. Aoife said she saw God in a dream, and she said He told her the devil lived in Pandora, and that he'd lead us all down a path of debauchery that would cost us all our places in Heaven at God's side. Aoife prayed night and day for intervention, to ensure the young girls didn't lose their places at God's feet. She was most worrited for thee, and thy unborn babe."

Hope felt rage rise inside her, eclipsing her earlier anger and hurt at Eldon. When she looked at him for permission, he nodded, and for the first time since their arrival, she saw compassion come back into his eyes. "I trusted you," she said angrily to Emma, who shrank under her glare. "You were the first friend I made after my rescue." Her glare turned to Daisy, who shivered. "And yet, the both of you let your prudishness cost us all our places here! Now we have to go back to Earth, and I know my father is just itching for the chance to get his hands on me! I'm going to probably be dead within the first twenty-four hours of getting back to Kings Cross, and how will I and my unborn baby be saved then? Have you idiots any idea of just what the hell you've done?"

Aoife opened her mouth, but Eldon cut her off. "No," he said, and now the compassion was much clearer. "The rest of you haven't lost your places." He took a deep breath. "All of that when we got here was a test," he told them. "Well, there was a bit of annoyance as well, but the majority of it was a test to see how you'd react to our way of life. I didn't mean for the test to be so harsh, but the council insisted, because they knew, from the moment we arrived, that there'd be trouble. So I had to be the way I was to see who was worthy of staying, and who wasn't. Aoife, Emma and Daisy failed, spectacularly.

The rest of you are free to go, and yes, you're all allowed to speak to each other, and to the staff."

Mia let out a sigh of relief. "Thank God," she said fervently, before a wicked glint entered her eye. "If my future husband dresses like some of the men we saw on our first day, I'd be jumping his bones for all to see." This sally released some of the long-held tension, and Hope laughed with the others as they left the study, but despite her levity, she felt fresh hurt and betrayal, this time at Emma and Daisy. Still, she was relieved that Eldon had only been testing them, and she found, as she followed her friends to the luxurious garden they'd glimpsed two days ago, that she really didn't mind as much as she'd thought. It meant that the real Eldon had been the one she'd first met on Earth, and it also meant she and her friends could stay. It was worth it, she thought, to be given the chance to live a new life, and despite her lingering sadness, she knew she couldn't wait to see what the future had in store for her now.

Chapter 9

ope snapped awake, heart pounding, eyes wide as she scanned her room. She couldn't see anything out of the ordinary, but her senses warned her there was something amiss. Moments later, her fears were confirmed when Aoife stepped out of the shadows, her face set. "What the hell are you doing here?" Hope demanded, clutching her blankets tightly to her.

"I'm getting you out of here," the Irishwoman said firmly, and Hope felt her heart plummet to the soles of her feet when Aoife produced a gun. "I'm sorry," the older woman said, pointing the gun at the terrified girl. "This is for your own good." She fired, and all went dark.

When Hope woke next, she found herself tied up, slung over Aoife's shoulder like a sack of potatoes. Kick and writhe though she might, the Irishwoman's skill at a rope was too good, and Hope soon gave up. That didn't stop her from screaming as loudly as she could, despite the gag in her mouth, but it did nothing more than earn her a sharp slap on the bottom. "Stop that," Aoife hissed. "You don't want to draw attention, do you?"

Everything tilted crazily for a moment, before Hope found herself on her feet, and her eyes widened when she saw Aoife was now pointing the gun at her stomach. Tears of fright slid down her cheeks, soaking her gag, but her tied wrists prevented her from doing anything to protect the life of her unborn child. "That's better," Aoife said. "I don't want to bring harm to your babe, but if we get the wrong sort of attention, I'd rather the wee mite was dead, rather than being subjected to the torments that will come the moment he or she draws their first breath."

Hope bit her gag hard, wishing someone, anyone would come to her aid. But the city was silent; it was well after two in the morning, and Aoife had made good use of the shadows. And if anyone came ... Hope wanted to throw up. Her nausea must have shown on her face; Aoife sighed. "I'm doing this for your own good," she said sharply. "I don't want you or your babe subjected to endless tests to see if you're 'safe'! I'd rather you raise that baby in safety on your own world. You don't belong here, child, and neither does your baby. I'm taking you home, and you'll be able to raise your child in peace, without anyone trying to claim him or her! Don't you want to see your son or daughter grow to maturity, to raise babies of his or her own?"

Hope bit the gag again, and when she felt the fabric tear, she gnawed at it until she could speak. "My father is waiting on the other side," she said sharply. "If I fall into his hands again, he'll never let me go! And if my child is a girl, he'll abuse her the way he abused me all my life! I'd rather be dead than let my father get my hands on me or my baby!"

Aoife sighed. "Your father is probably a good man, who's been under a little stress," she said. "He surely can't be as bad as you make him out to be." She shook her head. "No matter. When we're back on Earth, I'll arrange to have you transported safely to anywhere in the United Kingdom you wish to go, and I'll arrange to have you wed to a man who'll raise that child like it's his own." She pointed the gun at Hope's stomach again. "Since you won't be gagged, I'll untie you and let you walk on your own. But if you so much as blink in the direction of anyone, I'll make sure that child never draws his or her first breath."

Faced with the choice of losing her child or her freedom, Hope had no other option but to concede. "Fine," she said angrily, as Aoife untied her. "But that's not going to prevent people from seeing what's happening. We stand out like dog's balls--" Stars exploded in her vision, and by the time she could see again, her jaw throbbed like fury. Aoife glared at her.

"You watch your tongue," she snarled, "or so help me God, I'll kill you and that baby!"

Knowing she had lost, Hope rolled her eyes and kept her mouth shut. But as Aoife prodded her into motion, the young woman knew it was going to be hard for her captor to find the right train that would take them back to Earth. Not that Aoife would let her fall into Pandoran hands; the Irishwoman would kill the three of them before suffering capture, and silent tears of heartbreak slid down Hope's cheeks for quite a while.

Chapter 10

The station, like the rest of the city, was quiet, and as Aoife and Hope entered the grand concourse, the younger of the two felt more hopeless with every step that took her away from her new home and back towards her old home. No matter Aoife's promises, Hope knew no force on earth would stop her father when he found out she was still alive. And since Aoife was a great believer in family ties, Hope knew she'd try and find James the moment the two women returned to Earth - if they did. For Eldon had never told them what train they'd come in on, and as they looked at the departure board, which displayed trains and destinations in an unfamiliar language. Hope felt a very small amount of confidence come back.

Aoife, on the other hand, wasn't feeling the same way, and her face was grim as she studied the board. Then she pointed to a line of text with a blue and white planet next to it. "Earth," she said confidently. "That will be the train to get us home again." She grabbed Hope's wrist and towed her onwards, and the younger woman let herself be lead, hoping someone would stop them before they got on the train that would take them back.

But the ticket barriers were open at this time of night, and the one Pandoran who saw them sleepily waved them through, yawning widely. Hope felt sorry for him, having to pull a nightshift, but before long, she was feeling sorry for herself when Aoife confidently led them to the platform where, as Hope had feared, the train to Earth was waiting. She wanted to pull free, to scream for aid, but there was no one else on the platform, and she knew, even if someone did see them, that Aoife would have her shot dead in seconds.

The train was as empty as the station had been, and Hope felt new tears slide down her cheeks as Aoife got them seated well away from the doors. The train looked similar to the one that had brought them all to Pandora days ago, and Hope's heart sank as she recognised it - this was the same train, or a similar model, and Hope wanted to be sick again. All her hopes for freedom were being dashed one by one, and she clenched her fists as the doors shut. Before long, the train was moving, and Hope stared blindly out the window as the night-dark countryside passed them by. She could take no pleasure in the jewel-spangled, jet black sky, and as they climbed out of the valley and towards the tunnel, she cursed Aoife as bitterly and passionately as she knew how.

"Stow it," the Irishwoman told her sternly. "I won't have you snifflin' and feelin' sorry for yourself. This is for your own good, and if you were my daughter, I would have boxed your ears for bein' so sulky. I'm doing this to save you and your baby from hell, and if you don't stop your blubberin', I'll put you over my knee and give you a good spanking."

"Don't tell me what to do," Hope snapped. "You've got no right to tell me how to feel; I'm almost an adult, and I have every right to be sad!"

Aoife looked like she was ready to turn Hope over her knee right then and there, but soon the train entered the tunnel, and the Irishwoman shrugged. "Suit yourself," she said curtly, as the lights flashed past. "I'll be making sure your husband is a man who'll teach you to sit up straight and be grateful for the good life I'm leading you to. Or I can look up your father and let him deal with you. Either way, you'll be cured of your sulks soon enough, even if it means you won't be able to sit down for a week. Now shut up!"

Hope rolled her eyes, but resisted the urge to give the older woman the finger, instead turning her gaze to the window. She couldn't recall the moment when they'd made their transfer to the train that had delivered them to Pandora, but she did recall how everything had blurred around them for a moment, before time and space had settled again. She tensed, wondering if her argument with Aoife had caused her to miss that moment, and her dread grew as the train sped on. Resigned to her fate, she continued cursing the woman who had once been her friend, praying for the powers that be to visit on the Irishwoman the same fresh hell she was inflicting on the younger woman.

Chapter 11

After what seemed like an eternity, the train emerged from the tunnel, and Hope's eyes widened, before a huge smile crossed her face. Whether it was divine intervention, or Aoife's mistake, fate had been kind and had brought them back to Pandora. Aoife's were also wide, but with horror, and her face contorted like an animal's as the train approached Isonor station. "

No!

"she screamed, grabbing Hope's arm as the younger woman got up. "

NO!

"

Hope yanked her arm free and ran for the doors, but Aoife seized her hair and flung her to the floor. "

No!

"she screamed again, as she aimed the gun for Hope. It seemed to be the only word she could say, and it was Hope's turn to scream as she covered her head.

Then the doors opened, and the weight pinning her down was lifted. Friendly arms helped her to her feet, and she let out a sigh of relief when she saw Aoife firmly in the hands of Pandoran police. At least, their dark blue uniforms proclaimed them to be official in some way, and Aoife screamed incoherently as silver cuffs were slapped on her wrists and ankles. She twisted and thrashed, still screaming, as she was led off the train, and Hope sighed in relief once more as her own rescuer helped her off. "Thank you," she said to the young woman, who also wore a dark blue uniform. Too late she realised the Pandoran might not understand her, but the woman smiled at her.

"You're welcome," she said, her words pleasantly accented. "It appears the

ullu ka patta

misread the sign, or she forgot that you need a Pandoran on board with the skill to manipulate space-time to deliver any Earth guests back to their own land." She shook her head. "No matter. She is in custody now, and she will not get her hands on you again."

Hope sighed in relief. "I hope not," she said fervently.

The policewoman gave her a reassuring smile. "Our prisons are far more secure than anything you Earth people could devise," she said, as she helped Hope into a dark blue and silver car. "Even the most determined of criminals will have a very hard time getting out, and the ullu ka patta

will soon learn her wiles will be no match for the guards there. And we've devised punishments that will crack the toughest of inmates. I doubt the

ullu ka patta

will last long."

Hope wondered what that phrase meant, but as the car started up and headed for Eldon's mansion, she decided she was better off not knowing for now. It was enough to know Aoife was behind bars, and if the Pandoran policewoman's words were anything to go by, the Irishwoman was in for the fresh hell Hope had prayed for. Oddly, that made her feel better, and just the

tiniest

bit smug.

The mansion was in pandemonium when the police car pulled up, and Hope was soon swamped by her worried friends, all of whom had been terrified at waking up and see-ing her gone. Emma and Daisy - who'd been confined to their rooms prepatory to their return to Earth - had consequently been removed to the local jailhouse, and were now, so Penny said, being interrogated as to Aoife's plans. Neither woman had cracked yet, but Penny had the feeling it wouldn't be long before one or the other finally confessed to their part in the kidnapping.

Eldon, who looked as rumpled as any man going through a sleepless night, firmly intervened when he saw how tired Hope was. "That's enough," he said authroritatively. "The girl needs her sleep; you can ask her all the questions you want when she's got some rest."

This effectively quelled the relief, and Hope gave her friends a tired smile as they all trooped back inside. She was still worried that one of her former friends might try something else, but the glint in Eldon's eyes said he'd tear apart the next person who brought harm to her, and this made Hope feel more assured. And very thankful Eldon was on her side. She didn't want to be Aoife, Emma or Daisy when the Pandoran man got his hands on them.

Chapter 12

No further incidents took place, but Eldon confined the women to the mansion, and detailed his staff to keep a close eye on them, Hope especially. For all that Officer Jhansi had assured Hope Pandoran jails were frightfully secure, no one in the mansion felt safe, especially when it came out that Aoife had capitalised on the staff's one weakness - their eagerness to please. "Design flaw," Eldon confessed to Hope, as they walked through the garden that afternoon. "My fault; I wanted to enable them to be as useful as possible. That's how Aoife got through to them."

"You weren't to know," Hope assured him. "But it scares me how easily she managed to convince them to let her out!"

"Oh, love." Eldon rubbed a tired hand over his face. He hadn't shaved, and silver showed amongst the stubble on his cheeks. "Believe me, I've been doing nothing but kicking myself ever since last night. But if you want to add to the castigation, be my guest." A cheeky glint in his eye belied his weariness, and Hope smiled.

"I'm not giving you a hard time," she assured him. "I'm just scared how it happened so easily."

"The staff were told, in the wake of my little test, to treat all of you, barring those three, as honoured guests," Eldon told her. "Because of their programming, they obeyed my request, but I'd neglected to specifically exclude Aoife, Emma and Daisy from that list. Which is my fault; I forgot that they don't exclude anyone unless I specifically name names to be excluded. Not a mistake I'll be making again, I can assure you. I'm also going to upgrade the staff's programming to make them a

teeny

bit more skeptical, so that if this sort of thing should ever occur again, they'll have the good sense to come to me and make sure they're supposed to be doing the thing that's asked of them."

Hope sighed in relief. "Good," she said. "I won't lie," I'm still scared. I know none of those three can get out, but I'm worried they worked over any of the other women in the interim before this happened."

"Not a bit of it," Eldon assured her. "Mia was the one who told me the rest of the group don't subscribe to those mad-women's ideals. And I hate to be the bearer of bad news, but Emma and Daisy

are

as fervent as Aoife, even if they didn't show it so much until the manure hit the spinning blades. That's why they're being so stubborn, but no one else agrees, even if some of the more mature ladies are still getting used to seeing silver people in the buff." He grinned at this last, and Hope laughed.

"I didn't want to pry," she admitted, "but I did notice the men ... well, they look like Ken dolls downstairs."

"My idea," Eldon confessed. "I'm no prude, and I don't have a problem with nudity. Buuuut... I didn't want my lady guests going a bit crazy at full frontal nudity from my male staff. And it wasn't out of a desire to protect non existent virtue. None of them are programmed to give into carnal lusts, but I figured I'd keep things

semi

decent. And yes, the female staff have the same treatment downstairs, but that's not something you'd notice rightaway unless you were

really

looking." He sighed, his good humour dissipating, and Hope squeezed his hand.

"Me too," she said.

Eldon returned her squeeze with almost painful force, but she didn't care; the sensation reminded her she was free, for the moment, and that Eldon would stand in the way of

any

future attempts to remove her against her will. She certainly didn't blame him for being scared, and they held hands just a little tighter as they made their way back to the house.

Chapter 13

The next few days were very nerve-wracking for every-one; Aoife, Emma and Daisy were still

resisting all attempts to get their motives out of them, and Hope lived in daily terror that one day she might find all three of them at her bedside, ready to try and take her away again. Worse, she feared they might succeed in getting her back to Earth if they could talk a regular Pandoran into making the switch when they got to the thin space-time barrier separating Earth and Pandora.

Finally, a week after the failed kidnapping, Officer Jhansi came back with some encouraging news; Daisy had been the first to crack, and she'd confessed that, if Aoife failed, she'd be the next to try and get Hope out of the mansion. Much to Hope's horror, it turned out Daisy had a far more personal connection to her; she was, in fact, James's half sister, and therefore Hope's aunt. James had, according to Daisy, talked his way out of jail for the attempted murder of his daughter, and Daisy had, effectively been spying on

Hope ever since. To make matters even worse, Daisy had been feeding information back to James about Pandora, and when it had come out that Pandora was real, Daisy, Aoife and Emma had come together to hatch the kidnapping plan.

"God be good," Penny said, horrified, as Officer Jhansi finished her explanation. "We were so lucky Aoife didn't know about needing a Pandoran on board to manipulate the barrier in the tunnel!"

"Indeed we were," Officer Jhansi - who preferred to be called just Jhansi - said. "And we've not told any of them, so even if Hope's sperm donor did make his way to Pandora, he'd be arrested and sent back via space craft, with all his memories wiped. As it is, Daisy will be getting her memories wiped, and once she's returned to Earth, she'll only recall Pandora as a very vivid hallucination. Once Aoife and Emma have likewise confessed, they'll be treated the same way."

"Fair enough," Hope said. "Though if I may be so bold, I don't believe in fairness for any of them. That's the pregnancy hormones talking, I'm sure, but right now, I feel Aoife and Emma deserve to be memory wiped and packed back to Earth without the chance to confess."

Jhansi nodded. "I understand," she told the distressed girl. "I've a daughter your age, and if the same happened to her, I'd be breathing fire hotter than a sun dragon. But we have a very strict code of justice, and all lawbreakers must be given the chance to confess their crimes before they're punished.

That was the law our council agreed to when they were given leave to settle on Pandora, and it's written into our very bones. We literally cannot break that law; it is physically impossible, and even if someone did manage to break it without suffering a painful and prolonged death, all Pandorans - native or otherwise - would be asked to leave immediately."

"Well, whoever's in charge doesn't muck about," Mia observed.

"No," Jhansi told her. "And believe me, it's better this way. Criminals get a chance to explain themselves, no matter how long it takes, and they get their chance to have their side of the story explained." She rose. "I have to get back," she said, "but if I hear anything more, I promise I will come to you immediately, or send one of my colleagues."

"I'm still worried," Hope confessed, as Jhansi left.

"Me too," Penny and Mia said in unison. The other women nodded silent agreement, and Hope cursed the three women who were making her first weeks on Pandora such a nightmare. This was not what she'd signed up for when she'd first boarded the train weeks ago, but at least Daisy was now out of the picture, her memories wiped and all knowledge of how to get to Pandora taken from her. She just hoped Aoife and Emma would soon follow suit, but that would depend on their willingness to fall into line now that one of their co-conspirators had been exiled back to Earth.

Chapter 14

Jhansi came back with some unwelcome news a few days later. "Emma has confessed, and will have her memories wiped," she told the group. "Aoife, however, insists she needs to see Hope first."

Hope tensed. Mia and Penny, who'd become her best friends over the last harrowing few weeks, put their hands on her shoulder. "Why?" Penny demanded.

"I don't agree with it any more than you do," Jhansi agreed. "But the law is the law; we have to fulfil all our prisoners' requests. It's another rule we were told to agree to in order to live here."

"I can't see her," Hope said desperately. "I know you said your jail is locked up tighter than Fort Knox, but there's no telling what

the hell she might do when she sees me?"

"There are guards around her 24/7," Jhansi assured her. "And we have plenty of ways to ensure inmates can't harm those who come to see them. I know you don't want to see her again after what she did to you, but I will personally guarantee no harm will come to you."

This last part had the meaning of a sacred oath, and just for a moment, Jhansi's green eyes glowed as she spoke those last words. Hope felt goosebumps rise on her skin; Jhansi had clearly put her life on the line to guarantee the younger woman's safety, and though her fears weren't entirely erased, she did feel better. "Alright," she said.

Aoife didn't look like a prisoner, sitting on the other side of the inpenetrable shield placed between her and Hope. It looked like glass, but when Hope gave it an experimental push, it felt stronger and harder than steel. "Nothing and no one can get through that," Arjun assured her. Jhansi had been unable to be present due to an unexpected issue at the station, but Arjun had willingly sworn a similar oath of protection, and Hope felt better. But the glitter of rage in Aoife's eyes kept her on edge, and the girl placed a protective hand over her stomach. No morning sickness had as yet assailed her, but she felt very nauseous as Aoife's eyes went greedily to the hand covering the small, but growing life inside the girl she'd tried so hard to kidnap.

"Eyes front," Arjun snapped, and Aoife jerked as if stung. Her eyes reluctantly left Hope's belly, and the girl shivered. She wasn't scared of whatever Arjun had done to keep Aoife on the straight and narrow; she was scared of the fresh rage in the older woman's eyes. "And kill the hostility," the Pandoran officer added. "The girl is under my personal protection; I will give my life to ensure her safety and the safety of her unborn child."

Aoife sneered. "No protection is going to save you," she said. "I've got someone very dear to me waiting at the station."

Hope went rigid. "

Dad?

" she exclaimed, horrified. Arjun put a protective hand on her shoulder, and she calmed down, feeling an unexpected, but not unwelcome burst of warmth from the contact. "What the hell is he doing here?" the girl demanded in a more steady voice.

"He came here as soon as Daisy fed the information to him," Aoife told her. "Of course, it must have taken him some time to work out

how

to actually cross over, since

no one

has seen fit to tell

me

that!"

"That knowledge is forbidden to

khange khodah

like you," Arjun said coldly. "I have no idea how that

come mierda

found his way here, but I promise you, he is already being dealt with as we speak."

Aoife glared, but Hope felt nothing but relief. Jhansi would not be kind to James, of this she was certain, and while the inflexible Pandoran code would forbid any outright acts of malice against an offworlder, Hope had the sneaking suspicion James would be in for a

hell

of a hard time. "Dad can't hurt me, and neither can you," Hope said, as several things clicked into place about Aoife's demeanour. "And you will

never

get your hands on your great-grandchild."

"How the hell did you...?" Aoife cut off, her glare redoubling. "You needn't think a simple mindwipe will stop me

or

your father! That child is

family!

You have no right to keep him or her from us!

That is my great-grandchild in there, and I will do all I can to get my hands on them, even if I have to cut the blasted brat from your belly!

"

"And we're done here," Arjun said sharply, pressing a button on his sleeve cuff. The shield immediately turned dark as an alarm blared outside. Hope went white, but Arjun squeezed her shoulder, calming her once more. "I've called for an imme-diate mind wipe," he told her. "Jhansi will have explained how we can't just mind wipe people at will, save for exceptional circumstances, such as a confession, or a direct threat. The

khange khodah

is going to get a mind wipe, and when she returns to Earth, she won't recall

anything

about Pandora, let alone that it exists. Her accomplices will not recall much about it, nor will the

come mierda

who dared to try and breach our defences. He is already being prepared for an immediate mind wipe and exile, and like his mother, he will not even know Pandora exists."

Hope let out a long sigh of relief. "But doesn't that go against your code?" she asked.

"It would under normal circumstances," Arjun admitted with a smile as he helped her to her feet. "However, I've been in contact with Jhansi the whole time we were here, and she's informed me he has made several very credible threats to your person. I won't go into details, but they were very similar to what the

khange khodah

threatened you with."

"You're going to have to tell me what those words mean one day," Hope said, still rattled, but relieved enough to make a small jest.

Arjun chuckled. "One day," he promised. "Right now, I feel obliged to escort you to the break room for a nice, bracing cup of tea. The

khange khodah's

mind wiping will take a bit longer, and once she is returned to Earth along with her son, I'll escort you home."

"I think that sounds like a wonderful idea," Hope said fervently, feeling that, for the first time since her kidnapping, the nightmare was finally close to being over.

Chapter 15

It was late afternoon by the time Aoife and James had been exiled back to Earth, but not until nightfall was it deemed safe for Hope to return home. Arjun and Jhansi personally escorted her back, and Jhansi all but fell over herself apologising. "If I'd had any idea Daisy was feeding all she knew back to that

come mierda,

I'd have broken the law and wiped her right down to the very basics of her being," she said, shaking her head. "I had no

idea

she was as much of a weasel as her accomplices."

"I had the feeling something like that was going to happen when you couldn't make it," Hope admitted. "But at least they're no longer contendors."

"Not anymore," Jhansi assured her. "Emma and Daisy will, of course, only recall Pandora as a dream, and their memories of the place will fade over time. James and Aoife, on the other hand, won't even

know

there's such a place as Pandora. Even should it get men-
tioned, they'll just stare blankly and wonder what the hell
Emma and Daisy are talking about."

Hope sighed. "I'm just so glad it's finally over," she said. "I've
felt as though I've been doing nothing since fret ever since
Aoife tried to kidnap me." She wasn't going to refer to that
horrible woman as her grandmother, and Jhansi gave her a
lopsided smile that suggested she knew what was going on
in the girl's mind.

"I don't blame you," she said. "We value family very highly
here on Pandora, and for good reason. Every baby that sur-
vives birth is very precious to us, so you can imagine how
relieved we were when the council agreed in principle to
Eldon's idea."

"How long has it been since a baby survived birth?" Hope
asked carefully.

"Sixteen years," Jhansi said, her smile turning sad. "My
daughter was the last born beofre the disease really took
hold. And she was a baby conceived of one of the Earth
women who came to us unofficially to try and turn the disease's tide. The woman herself passed delivering the child,
but her last words begged for me to take the baby as my
daughter and raise her, and though I was grieved at the
mother's loss, I fulfilled that duty. But my daughter, sadly, is
barren, as was discovered when she took ill a few months ago.

She survived, but the disease had made her as infertile as all the surviving women."

Hope sucked in a shocked breath. "And you say no baby has survived birth since then?" she said, horrified.

Jhansi nodded. "And none of the Earth women who came to us the first time are alive," she said. "They all succumbed to the disease, and the last one died only a few months ago. She'd had multiple miscarriages, and the doctors believe it was those that ultimately killed her, and not the disease."

"That's why Eldon wants to make your venture an official one," Arjun said, giving Jhansi's hand a squeeze and winning a watery smile from her. "This way, you are all protected, and your children will be protected as well. We may need to do some tests on each baby that is born, but no matter what their genes, they will not be separated from their mothers. The council isn't as hard as that."

"Thank God for that," Hope said. "I'm still rattled after all that happened, and I really didn't want to face the prospect of losing my baby to someone else's wiles."

"It won't happen," Arjun promised. "No matter what, all babies born will stay with their mothers, and they'll be given the same rights as native born Pandorans. That I can promise you, and you already know we take the matter of promises very

seriously."

Hope nodded. And as the car approached Eldon's mansion, she finally felt at peace. Anyone who wished to bring harm to her or her baby was out of the picutre, and once the council had formally signed off on Eldon's plan, life would truly begin here on the planet Hope already felt was more like a home to her than Earth had ever been.

Chapter 16

It took a few more days before the matter of Aoife and her schemes were finally wrapped up, and Hope was saddened to hear that her grandmother had committed suicide as soon as she'd been delivered back to Earth. She didn't grieve the woman herself, but the relationship she might've had had Aoife not been so determined to seize her great-grandchild. As it was, she was dead, and while Hope was sad, deep down she was relieved. Now Aoife would never put two and two together despite her memory loss.

James, on the other hand, had not been so easy to mind wipe, and while the authorities' hands were tied, they did ensure James would never make it to the portal between worlds; his image and DNA were broadcast far and wide, and every passenger boarding the train to Pandora from Earth would be scanned rigorously. Hope had faith in the process, but it still scared her to know James still remembered Pandora, and for the next few days, she lived in worry, until news came to her a few days after Aoife's passing; James had drunk himself into unconsciousness, and died on the way to hospital from alcohol poisoning. There was no way to determine if the over drinking had been accidental or on purpose, but either way, his threat was now removed, and Hope found herself breathing just a bit easier.

Emma and Daisy, in the meantime, were slowly losing their recollections of Pandora, but neither had any inclinations to try and get to a place they firmly believed was just a figment of their imagination, but another week passed before their threat was also deemed wrapped up; two Pandorans had gone across the barrier between worlds, and the two women had, so the reports ran, laughed when told where the Pandorans had come from, calling them crazy and threatening to have them locked up. Hope had to laugh when the news came to the mansion. "At least now they won't think about trying anything funny," she said.

"No," Jhansi agreed. "I thought that might cheer you up. And I'm truly sorry it's taken this long for things to finally come to an end. We had to be sure Emma and Daisy would laugh off any mentions of Pandora, and their threats to try and have two of our own committed was the proof we needed. Our people did do full scans of the women to make sure it wasn't just an act, but each has well and truly forgotten Pandora ever existed. They won't be trying any tricks any time soon."

Hope sighed in relief. "Thank God for that," she said fervently. "I feel as though so much bloody time has been wasted with all this nonsense!"

"I know," Jhansi said, squeezing her hand. "But it's finally over, and now you and your friends can meet the council and learn first hand of just what awaits you. And you've all been given leave to explore the city to your hearts' content. The danger is over, and no one will be coming through the portal to bring harm to any of you."

Life finally settled down after that for the women from Earth, and they threw themselves into exploring Isonor from end to end, and top to bottom. Nothing was said of the last few weeks, and Hope was very glad to put it behind her as she wandered the streets, gawking at all the sights, sounds and smells that greeted her. Isonor did remind her of Earth in some ways, but always, the Pandorans shattered that illusion. But Hope no longer minded; she was glad Isonor was so different. Reminders of Earth were still a little painful, but now that the nightmare of her attempted kidnapping was well and truly wrapped up, she knew the pain would fade over time.

And there was so much to look forward to; as the days passed, Hope found her old excitement coming back as she wandered the city. Eldon had assured them that the council was coming to a decision about the women from Earth, and he promised that as soon as he knew what it was, he'd inform them. But, he'd added, no matter what the council said, the women would be welcome to make their home here, even if the council officially turned down the proposed venture

Eldon hoped to launch. This had put everyone's mind at ease, Hope's especially. She herself was beginning to feel she'd be happy to stay in the city, although the lands beyond Isonor were incredibly tempting. She made a vow to herself that if the council turned down the proposed venture, she'd go visit some of the lands outside Isonor and see what other wonders the planet had to offer. If Isonor was any indication, the rest of Pandora surely had to be just as exhilirating.

Chapter 17

A week later, Eldon informed the women it was time to meet the council. "They want to give their verdict in person," he said, but his face betrayed neither relief nor chagrin. This put more than one woman slightly on edge, but to Hope, it was almost a relief to be worrying about the council and not about her own fate at the hands of crazy family members. Still, she was just as nervous as her friends, and she hoped that this turn of events would be the harbinger of good news and not bad.

The council hall was enormous, lit by a million floating lights that hung without support in the cavernous space. Full length stained-glass windows depicted scenes of war, peace, famine and prosperity, and Hope gasped when she saw dragons, unicorns, pegasi, mermaids, and other mythical creatures depicted in the designs. People of unearthly beauty also figured prominently in the windows, and when the group reached the dais where the council waited, they could all see where the Pandorans had got their eyes from.

Five chairs stood arranged on the dais, all of equal height, and on those chairs sat the five members of the council. They had the cat eyes of all Pandorans, but each of them had a different colour - deep blue, forest green, sea green, sky blue, and deep voilet. Hope soon saw why this was so - behind each councillor stood a creature of unearthly beauty, similar to those in the stained glass windows, and she soon saw that each creature had the same eye colour as the man or woman they stood behind. And behind

them

were the fantasy creatures also depicted in the windows. A massive golden dragon rested its head on the floor, the rest of it presumably outside, and there was also a unicorn, a pegasus, a centaur, and a mermaid, who could not be mistaken for anything else with her scaled blue-green skin and the seashells that covered her bare breasts. Hope and her friends had, of course, become used to the casual attitude towards modesty, so the mermaid's state of undress bothered them not at all.

"The five people behind the dais are the five heads of the elven clans who gave us leave to settle here," Eldon explained in a low murmur to the group. "You can probably tell by the colouring, but we've got the sun elves, moon elves, sea elves, sky elves and forest elves. The creatures behind them are, well, their gods, in a way, and each clan draws its power from the five creatures who created them. Each councillor is linked to his or her corresponding elven leader, and they serve for life. Heirs are very carefully chosen to ensure they follow the precepts laid down by the elves, and blood doesn't always necessarily guarantee a succession."

Hope shook her head in wonder. "I'm turned all on my head again," she confessed in a whisper.

Eldon chuckled. "They don't bite, at least not on the first date," he teased, and Hope giggled.

Presently, they reached the dais, and the sun councillor rose, bowing deeply. "We give you greeting," he said. "I am Jaiden, and I welcome you to Pandora. I understand things have been a little... tense, and I sincerely apologise for any distress you have suffered at the hands of those who wished you harm."

"That's the understatement of the century," Penny muttered, and a ripple of laughter passed over the dais. Once the mirth had settled, Jaiden then introduced his fellow councillors; Zayn, who stood for the moon elves, Arian, who stood for the sea elves, Jahan, who stood for the forest elves, and Meera, who stood for the sky elves. Then their counterparts were introduced; sun elf leader Navi, moon elf leader Jaya, sea elf leader Satya, forest elf leader Manav, and sky elf leader Nayan.

With introductions made, chairs were brought for the women, and they sat gratefully. "Eldon has explained the situation to you," Jaiden said. "I will therefore not elaborate, save to say this; you are all honoured guests here. No matter the path you choose to take, you will never be exiled back to Earth. I am given to understand some of you led lives there that were less than ideal, and I promise you here and now, you will never be made to go back there again. You are, as of this moment, free to roam Pandora as you wish, and our five elven chieftains have given you the run of the place, so to speak."

Zayn then took up the narrative. "We have agreed to Eldon's idea," he said. "We were very reluctant to do so, given that Jhansi's daughter was the only Earth child to survive. All other babies died, as did the first group of women who came here. But Eldon believes that if you all are given the same protection as native Pandorans, you will stand a better chance of survival, as will your unborn babies. I for one am not very keen on the idea, but we agreed that it is, at least, worth pursuing. Therefore, you will be accorded the same rights and priviledges as native Pandorans, and the children born to you will also be treated as citizens. We are not ready to declare you citizens, as that is a process that will take some time, and we feel you have all been through enough. But though you are not official Pandorans, the instructions have gone out; all residents of Isonor, as well as the lands beyond, have been informed of your somewhat irregular status, and any who mistreat you for any reason will feel the full force of the law, just as if the insult had occurred to a native Pandoran."

"And your children will be treated the same," Arian added. "As you may have had explained to you, any children born of you will be tested to determine if they have inherited the gene for the disease which has so sadly ravaged our ranks. No matter how they, or you, test, no one will be cast out, but will instead be given care to the fullest measure. No one will be stinted, or treated as if they are leprous. We did not treat the first group of Earth women that way, and Jhansi's daughter is treated exactly the same as if she'd been born here, regardless of her barren state. But, despite the testing that must be undertaken when your babies are born, you will not

be robbed of them, and you will be able to care and raise them. No mother will be separated from her child; on this you have our personal word, and you know by now that it is impossible for a Pandoran to break their word."

"Be welcome," the councillors then said as one, and Hope let out a long sigh of relief, tears streaming freely down her cheeks as she and her friends shared a fervent group hug. The councillors and their elven counterparts then came down from the dais to properly welcome the women to Pandora, and as the celebrations truly got underway, Hope finally had the feeling she'd well and truly come home.

Chapter 18

The celebrations went well into the evening, during which the now-unofficial Pandoran women were told they were free to decide what they wished in regards to their future. All were assured that, no matter what they chose, they'd be free to live on Pandora for the rest of their lives, and they'd be treated as Pandorans in all but name, as would any of their children should they choose not to participate in Eldon's venture. This was very reassuring to the women, especially Hope, Annie, Lola, and Emily, all of whom were pregnant. "Thank god," Annie said, sighing in relief. "I didn't want to be handin' my child over to them to see if they'd be 'safe'!"

"I don't think they'd be handed over willy-nilly," Lola assured her. "Well, that's the hope, anyway. And it wouldn't matter if they were 'safe' or not. Jhansi's daughter was conceived on Earth, and she's treated just the same for all that the poor girl's barren from the disease."

Hope nodded. "I think our children will be treated the same," she promised the other expecting women. "And if it fails, we and our children will be protected in whatever fashion the Pandorans see fit. I don't think we're going to be shunned or kicked out because our children turn out to be barren."

"How do you suppose the disease ever manifested in those first women who came here?" Emily wondered.

"I've no idea," Hope said. "But maybe Pandoran medicine has come a long way since Saanvi was born. If it does become prevalent in any of us, I'm sure they'll be able to intervene more swiftly and treat it before it can become a serious problem."

But as the women rejoined the celebrations, Hope admitted to nerves. She hadn't yet broached the subject of what exactly would happen should the disease attack her or any of her friends. They'd all been assured their fates as unofficial Pandorans was secure either way, but Hope couldn't quite quell the dart of nerves that went through her heart.

Life soon settled for the newly minted Pandoran women, and before long, they were finding their way through the vast wonders that the lands beyond Isonor had to offer. Though they couldn't find matches with any of the elven races, due to the elves not wanting the disease to come to them - and for good reason - there were plenty of Pandoran men who clamoured for their attention. However, the men were very respectful of the newcomers, and if they were turned down, they never pushed the issue, but accepted it and moved on. From this, Hope guessed that, despite the dire situation which would easily see the Pandoran humans wiped out in a generation or two, the men weren't desperate enough to force their attentions on anyone who wasn't interested. "We are desperate," Arjun explained, when Hope broached the subject to him. "But we'd never force ourselves on any of you. We'll take you out for as many coffees as you desire, but we'd never see it as anything more than a coffee outing, unless any of you want it to be more."

"Oh good," Hope said. "I had a feeling that was the case."

Arjun smiled. He was actually rather good looking, Hope admitted to himself, but despite her interest, she wasn't sure if she wanted to pursue any romantic attachments as yet, given how almost all the men in her life had failed her in one fashion or another. Idly, she wondered what the father of her baby was doing right now, but dismissed the thought; her unborn child would probably have a few half-sisters and brothers in the womb by now, but as for the father... Hope pushed him from her mind. He could do as he wanted, but at least one child, Hope promised, would have a better life than the unborn siblings who'd face a much less pleasant life. "You know," she said, snapping out of her reverie, "I think coffee dates - well, tea dates, in this case - are the way of the future for now."

"I understand," Arjun said, inclining his head. "I will take you out on as many tea dates as you desire until you're ready to make them something more. I'm a patient man, and you need not fear I will force any unwanted desires on you. Your father has left many scars on your heart and soul, as has the father of your child, and it would be remiss of me to inflict further distress on you until some of those wounds have healed."

"Thank you," Hope said, giving him her best smile. "With that said, I think another tea is in order to seal the deal."

"Done," Arjun said, gently tapping his empty cup against hers.

Chapter 19

Happiness turned to heartbreak, however, when Mia came down with the disease only weeks after the former Earth women had been welcomed to Pandora. Good nursing pulled her through, but when she was examined afterwards, she was discovered to be barren, much to the shock of all present. Her new husband, Abir, was just as stunned as she, but he refused to divorce her, stating that he cared deeply for her, and he would not put her aside. This eased some of Mia's pain, but the heartbreak showed clearly in her eyes every time Hope saw her, and her heart ached for her friend.

Penny was next to take ill, and it wasn't long before all of the former Earth women also became ill. Penny was one of the unfortunate casusalties, followed by Annie, Lola, and their unborn children. Emily survived, but lost her baby, much to the heartbreak of Agni, her new husband. Like Abir, Agni stuck by his wife's side, despite the pain of losing yet another precious life. Before long, Emily, Hope and Mia were the only survivors, but with Mia and Emily now being rendered barren,

Hope found all eyes were on her. She didn't blame everyone for being worried that she or her child might be the next to succumb, but all the same, she felt like a lab rat. Her baby had, against all odds, survived, but even so, it was a very tense time, and though Hope submitted to regular tests without complaint, she had the nasty feeling that, despite their strict code, the Pandorans were going to find a loophole in their promises not to separate her from her unborn child.

Arjun was very grim when she broached this towards the end of her pregnancy. "No one can find 'loopholes'," he said shortly. "It is literally impossible for us to break our word, either directly or indirectly." He sighed and gently stroked his wife's hair - they'd been married for two months, and Hope had found him to be a very satisfactory spouse. "But I understand your fear," he said. "If they try to take your child from you, I will personally hold them answerable. Your child is the very last chance we have of survival, but no one shall force him or her to become an 'incubator' for the next generation. You have my word on this."

Hope felt infinitely better, but the fear persisted despite her best efforts to rein it in. Arjun would, naturally, be the first to vehemently protest his veracity; being a Pandoran, he'd jump to the defence of his people in a heartbeat, and Hope couldn't help but wonder if he was lying in some way to try and make her feel better. It was all very well for him to promise to stand up to anyone trying to take her child from her, but he hadn't won her over fully. Hope, however, had the good sense to keep her mouth shut, and though it pained her to deceive her husband, she knew better than to broach further doubts to him. It would only get him angry, and Hope didn't want to risk another man turning on her. Her scars from James' treatment were still raw in many ways, but Arjun had, on the surface at least, proven himself to be an exemplary man, and Hope prayed, as she got ready for another test, that her fears were groundless. She didn't want to go on the run again, but if she had to, she was ready.

Chapter 20

In the early hours of the morning, almost nine months after arriving on Pandora, Hope went into labor. Fears for her baby's fate didn't make for an easy delivery, but the midwife was very stern with her, telling her to stop fretting. "Your baby won't come out if his or her mother isn't willing," she said curtly. "I suggest you stop interfering with the process." Her tone conveyed things might go badly for Hope if she didn't comply, and the girl grimaced between contractions. But she had no choice; her baby was past ready to be born. Setting her fear aside, she concentrated on the process at hand.

As the sky began to lighten, Hope gave birth to a healthy baby girl. The newborn was immediately whisked away after the cord had been cut, and though tired and in pain, Hope prayed the check up wouldn't take too long. But as she was cleaned and stitched up, no one returned with her baby, and her fears resurfaced. "Where's my baby?" she demanded of one of the nurses. "Please, where's my baby?"

"Your baby is being checked over," the nurse replied shortly. "Now be quiet; you don't want to upset your milk supply, do you?"

Thus quashed, Hope endured a nightmare few hours before her baby was finally brought to her. But even then, she had to wait for another few agonising minutes before she was finally allowed to hold her daughter, and everything melted away in the rush of love she felt as she looked on the tiny face. "She's beautiful," she murmured, her eyes filling with tears. "I can't believe it."

The nurse who'd brought her baby to her gave her a stern glance. "Stop crying," she said. "You have your baby now; why are you acting like a child? If you don't stop, I'll take her away until you can promise me you'll keep your emotions in check."

Hope took a deep breath. "I'm just glad she's alive," she said, forcing herself to calm down, since the nurse looked ready to snatch her daughter from her there and then.

The nurse sniffed. "I've half a mind to take her away," she warned. "You're behaving very badly."

It was on the tip of Hope's tongue to give an equally sharp reply, but since the conversation had drawn a few more nurses, all of whom were glaring at her, she refrained. "I'm sorry," she said meekly. At that moment, her baby began to stir, and, instinctively guessing what her daughter needed, Hope unlaced her nightgown one-handed. One of the nurses intervened before she could begin feeding her daughter. "No," she said. She produced a bottle and, with the air of one performing an unpleasant duty, handed it to the new mother. "Your child is very precious," the nurse told the shocked girl. "Until her tests have been completed, you'll be feeding her formula. Once it has been determined breastfeeding is safe, you'll be permitted to do so."

Her tone warned of dire consequences if Hope didn't comply and, feeling like she was nothing more than an incubator, Hope reluctantly gave the bottle to her daughter. Luckily the baby took to the bottle immediately, and Hope felt some of her bitterness fade away as she watched the tiny hands gripping the warm plastic. She was very careful to keep her face neutral, but it was very hard when the nurses all watched her like a hawk, ready to snatch her baby away at the first sign of emotion.

The feeding done, Hope gently wiped the baby's mouth and burped her, and soon, the tiny body in her arms settled into sleep once more. One of the nurses took the empty bottle. "You'll be feeding her every four hours," she instructed the new mother. "We'll have a crib moved in so you can keep her close to you, but be warned; you will be watched whenever you and the baby are together. If you're caught crying, or showing any untoward emotions, the baby

will

be removed from your care until you can prove to us you're ready to be an adult. You're a mother now; it's time to put all your childish emotions behind you."

This, Hope thought resentfully, was very unfair. But at least her baby was with her, for the time being, at least. Keeping a lid on her emotions would be very difficult, but if she could conceal her fears from her husband, she could easily put on a mask of meekness for these crotchety old goblins who ate rocks for breakfast and picked their teeth with the bones of small animals.

Besides,

she told herself, as the promised crib was rolled into her room,

they can't keep an eye on me 24/7.

Chapter 21

The nurses soon proved her wrong, and Hope had to learn very swiftly how to keep her face neutral whenever she and her daughter were together. The nurses, however, seemed to be very well trained in watching for even the slightest change in expression, and more often than not, Hope would have to ask very calmly and very politely to have her daughter returned to her. It didn't help that she had to do this in front of a number of several rather disapproving old vultures, and more often than not, they took their sweet time in bringing her daughter back to her, often leaving it until 24 to 48 hours later before the baby's crib was rolled back into the room. It seemed the only moments of privacy she had was when she was in the toilet or shower, but she knew she could never indulge in those stolen moments for long, lest she find her daughter's crib gone from her room again when she came out.

To make matters worse, she wasn't allowed to name her daughter, the implication being that this was the province of her husband. Arjun, however, had not been present for the baby's birth, and as Hope recovered and learned how to be a mother on her own, he never once stopped by the hopsital to see her, even though she was the mother of the first baby to survive birth in almost a generation.

Neither Mia nor Emily were permitted to visit, making the isolation even worse. Hope had to ask to be allowed to send them a message to let them know her baby had been delivered safely, and was thriving despite the extenuating circumstances her mother was going through. Thankfully the nurses delivered her message, and presented a message of congratulations from her friends and their husbands. Life was progressing well for them despite their barren state, and their husbands were treating them like queens. Hope had been praying for the same attention from her own husband, but as her discharge day approached, he never appeared, nor did he send word to congratulate his wife. Hope told herself he was busy doing police officer work, but even Jhansi and Saanvi had sent congratulations, and Jhansi was a full time police officer herself.

Discharge day soon came, and as Hope got ready, she thanked her lucky stars that she'd escape the never-ceasing vigil which was preventing her from fully expressing her emotions as a mother. But she kept her face calm as she finished signing her release forms, only for that calm to be shattered when she saw she was the only one being released; the default spot where her daughter's name would have gone was blank. It took all the strength she had to remain level-headed as she asked about her baby. "I've done all you asked of me," she said steadily, despite the renewed fears crawling in the pit of her stomach."

"You have," the head nurse said grudgingly. "But our orders are clear. The baby stays here pending a decision by the council."

Hope felt the blood drain from her face. "But they promised I wouldn't be separated from my child," she said, fighting to keep herself under control. "Arian himself promised on oath that I'd be allowed to care for and raise my daughter!"

"You will be allowed to care for and raise

a

daughter," the head nurse corrected her. "Your firstborn is now the province of the council, and her fate will be de-termined in time. You are free to go, but you will not be permitted to leave the city until it has been determined if the disease yet works in your system. If you prove to be fertile, you will be permitted to conceive another baby, and that baby will be free for you to raise and care for, once the requisite tests have been done."

"My firstborn is

not

a guinea pig!" Hope said, furious now. "What if she's inherit-ed the gene that causes the disease? What will you do then? Turn her out on the street and let her fend for herself? Or will you subject her to an autopsy after you've decided to kill her and see what can be salvaged should she turn out to be a carrier?"

"That is enough," the head nurse warned. "If you keep this up, you will be

immediately

escorted to the station and sent home!"

Hope gave a bitter laugh. "I see how it is," she said coldly. "Mia and Emma are treated like queens even though they're barren. I, on the other hand, am subjected to tests to see if I turn up barren, and my daughter is now the

property

of your

scumbag

council until they can determine for themselves if she's a good investment!" She drew herself up to her full height. "You can send me home if you want," she said. "That just proves your council are a bunch of liars, and that

no

Pandoran can be trusted to keep their word!"

"Leave," the head nurse told her. "You are no longer welcome here. And once I've finished speaking to the council, you will no longer be welcome on Pandora!"

"I'll go," Hope said, "but I won't be leaving without my daughter, I can promise you that." She turned and stalked out, tears streaming down her cheeks as she left her baby behind, subject now to the fate she'd prayed the tiny life would never be subjected to, her heart breaking with every step she took.

I

will

get you back,

she thought,

even if I have to tear the place down myself!

Outside, it was raining, and Hope shivered, painful memories of almost a year ago coming back to her, slamming her in the face with the full force of an express train going full speed. But she had no desire to throw herself into the nearest body of water; instead, a powerful need for justice drove her, and as she hurried through the wet streets, she already knew where she was going. And like the rain beating down on her head, she was ready to come down with the same force on the one man she'd thought she could trust above all others on this miserable planet.

Chapter 22

Hope only made it a few blocks before Jhansi found her. "You have to go," the policewoman told the girl, regret in every line of her body. "I'm so sorry; the council just passed a decree that you were to be escorted to the station and onto the next train bound for Earth.

Hope dug her heels in. "I'm not going without my daughter," she insisted. "I don't care
what
those prune-faced hags at the hospital say. That's
my
daughter there, and I won't have her become the latest experiment!
"

Jhansi had started to smile at the prune-faced comment, but the humour was quickly wiped from her face at Hope's last words. "Your daughter is going to be in the best car,e," she said. "Believe me; no matter what those 'prune-faced hags' told you, no harm will come to your daughter." Her face firmed. "But you won't be around to see her grow up. You've worn out the goodwill of the council by your behaviour, and their word is as law; if you're not on the next train to Earth, you'll be jailed."

"I'd rather be jailed than exiled," Hope snapped, hurt filling her. It wasn't like Jhansi to give her such a dressing-down as this; in all the time she'd known the policewoman, Jhansi had been nothing but supportive to her, and whenever she did tell someone off, she was much more polite than the blunt rudeness she was using with Hope now. "Everyone on this planet lied to me," the girl added, refusing to be budged. She'd make Jhansi drag her if need be! "I was told I wouldn't be separated from my daughter, but they're not letting her come home with me."

"Your daughter is in good hands," Jhansi insisted. "Believe me; she will come to no harm, and nothing will be done to her to cause her unnecessary pain. Now you must go, or I'll have no choice but to take you to the station and have you formally charged with trespassing."

"Then do it!" Hope snapped, long-suppressed tears finally filling her eyes. "That just proves you're the same as your precious council!"

Jhansi stiffened as if struck, but before Hope could take back her hasty words, the policewoman's face went rigid with anger. "Very well," she said through clenched teeth as she pulled out her baton and aimed at the girl. A blast of white light filled Hope's eyes, and then darkness claimed all her senses.

When next Hope woke, she found herself in a very spartan room. The floor was bare earth, and a narrow cot with a none-too-plump mattress, together with a cracked wash-stand were the only furnishings. A bucket in one corner served as a toilet, and from the smell of it, it hadn't been emptied, let alone cleaned, for some time. Hope wrinkled her nose in disgust as she got painfully to her feet, her body protesting the movement. Whoever had tossed her in here hadn't been too gentle; she was going to have bruises for days, and she groaned as she rubbed the back of her neck. It was still tender to the touch; Jhansi had not been kind, and Hope cursed the Pandoran policewoman for being as fickle and untrustworthy as her countrymen.

When I get out of here,

she vowed,

I'll make sure the whole damn

universe

knows that Pandorans can't be bloody trusted! I'll throttle the idiot who thought it was a good idea to rescue me the night I ran away from home! I was better off dead!

The door crashed open and Hope jumped. Jhansi stood in the doorway, two orderlies at her side. One carried a bowl of soup; the other held a glass of water. "Lunch," the policewoman informed her coldly. "Be thankful you're getting food; if anyone else was in charge of your care, they'd probably reduce your meals to one a day. Oh, and for the record, you're not to speak unless spoken to, not even to thank anyone who brings you your food. Do I make myself clear?"

Hope swallowed. "Crystal," she said.

Jhansi nodded. "Good," she said. She gestured to the orderlies, who put the food and water on the floor. "You'll be allowed an hour's exercise each day," the policewoman said. "But you will speak to no one, and you will do
all
as you are told. If you disobey in any way, I'll have you moved to the underground cells, and you won't like them one bit. They have a bad tendency to flood whenever the river rises, and it's been raining quite a lot lately." With this last salvo, she turned and left, slamming the door behind her, and Hope bit back the urge to curse as she lifted the bowl. The basic kindness of a spoon had been overlooked, but Hope didn't care, and she downed the soup eagerly, trying hard not to think about the suspect chunks of meat contained in the brown depths. It was decent enough, thankfully, and the glass of water did the trick to wash it down. Hope then set the bowl and glass on the floor next to the door, before

reluctantly using the rank bucket. Soap and water provided an alternative to toilet paper, and Hope made sure to wash her hands thoroughly afterwards.

But as she sat on the bed, watching the small patch of dark blue sky outside, she felt sick inside, cursing herself for her stupidity. Having lost everything, she knew she should've let Jhansi take her to the station. If she hadn't blown her stack, she'd likely be back on Earth by now. To be sure, Earth still wasn't a pleasant place, but as Hope sat on the bed, she felt it would be better than where she was right now.

Chapter 23

Hope wasn't sure how long she spent in the cell; time lost all meaning, and she soon found it hard to distinguish the difference between day and night. She never saw another soul during her time there, and in any case, she was forbidden from speaking to anyone unless they addressed her directly. Her dull grey prison uniform marked her as an outcast, so no one save Jhansi spoke to her. And even then, the policewoman was curt and to the point, making sure Hope knew how deeply she'd screwed up. The odd thing was, she most often did it in public, but whenever she came to the cell, she was civil, if not exactly warm. Hope didn't really care one way or the other; to her, Jhansi represented the worst Pandoran society had to give, and she wasn't inclined to view her one time friend as anything more than an enemy now.

A week, or maybe more, passed before Jhansi came to the door after breakfast. Normally it was one of the orderlies who collected the used dishes, and Hope was a little surprised. But renewed bittnerness swallowed that emotion as the policewoman ordered her curtly to her feet. She said no further word after that, and Hope followed her silently, head bowed. She could feel the gaze of other police officers on her, but to her continued relief, Arjun wasn't among them. She had no idea what her former husband was doing, but she considered herself fortunate he didn't have her in his care; there was no telling what he might do when they were alone. Hope didn't relish the idea of letting any man near her ever again.

Her thoughts were soon interrupted when Jhansi pushed open the door of the communal bathroom. "Get inside and shower," she directed. "There'll be clean clothes for you when you step out, and don't even think about complaining or muttering to yourself; I'll be right outside the shower door."

Hope bit her tongue hard enough to almost draw blood, but she did as she was told, and as the hot water cascaded over her hair and body, she felt a bit better for the first time since being forced to leave her daughter behind. She wondered how her lost baby was doing, but she knew better than to inquire of Jhansi, who'd probably give her yet another lecture. Hope finished her shower in renewed bitterness, and once she'd dried and dressed, this time in dark brown, Jhansi led her out of the bathroom and eventually, they emerged onto the street. Hope felt her heart sink in dismay, but she supposed the council had come to a decision regarding her fate; Earth would be waiting on the other side of the tunnel, and while she didn't relish going back to the place that had hurt her so much, she didn't relish the prospect of staying on Pandora any longer than was necessary.

However, when they got to the station, Jhansi stopped her and produced a blindfold. "I won't have you guessing where the entry point is," she said coldly. "The council have agreed not to mind wipe you, but that doesn't mean you can come here and try to steal a child that no longer belongs to you."

Hope finally snapped. "You know there's something more going on!" she said angrily. "That's why you've kept me locked away like a common criminal! You know what's happened to my daughter! And you also know she's not the first baby to taken from her rightful mother. Is that what you did to Saanvi's mother sixteen years ago!"

Jhansi went rigid. "You have no idea what happened when Saanvi's mother gave birth to her," she said through clenched teeth. "And if you don't want to be stung again, and this time thrown in the river to drown, you will keep your damned mouth shut! You have no idea of what is going on!"

"I do," Hope insisted. "And I won't be muzzled or locked away! Where is Saanvi's mother? And what happened to Emily's son? They all say she miscarried, but she told me he was almost old enough to survive!"

"You will say nothing more," Jhansi warned, pulling out her baton. "You speak of matters that are forbidden for the likes of you and me."

Hope stood her ground. "You know something is going on," she said, refusing to be budged. "And I will not rest until I get to the bottom of it!"

Jhansi glared at her. "Stop," she said. "Either you go in peace, or I knock you out and throw you in the river. Which is it going to be?"

Sensing how close she was to peril, Hope backed down. "I'll go," she said. "But I won't go blindfolded like a criminal. You have my word I won't try and find the way back, but neither will I stop my daughter when she decides to go looking for her mother! And when that day comes, I'll tell her the truth!"

"Your daughter will never leave Pandora," Jhansi said, her voice thin and tight with an anger Hope had never seen in her before. "She is Pandoran by birth, and she will never be permitted to go through the portal to Earth so her head can be filled with lies."

Hope snorted. "Try," she said. "Now get me on this train so I never
have to see any of your smug,
lying
faces again. Oh, and tell Eldon to get fucked. If he ever tries recruiting more women to be brood mares, he's going to find

it very hard to find anyone willing to come here and be used, then thrown aside like wet rags!"

Jhansi said nothing to this, but her face was black as thunder as she prodded Hope up the steps and into the station. The girl went passively, but she was seething with a rage equal to and surpassing Jhansi's. With her memories intact, she could spread the news far and wide; Eldon would have to cast his net elsewhere to find willing broodmares for whatever twisted experiment the Pandorans had going on.

Chapter 24

When the train emerged from the tunnel, Hope was shocked to see, instead of the familiar English countryside, a dimly lit station that looked like it had seen better days. She wondered if Jhansi had put her on the wrong train by accident, but dismissed that idea; the policewoman had been very thorough, and had confirmed with the station staff which train Hope needed to get on.

Yet, as the train slowed down and stopped, Hope had the nasty feeling she'd just been sent to a much worse place than Earth and Pandora combined. Still, there seemed to be little choice in the matter; the doors slid open smoothly, and Hope stepped reluctantly from the train, shivering in the draft as the train sped away from the stations, the rails' "singing" fading away into an eerie silence as the train vanished through the tunnel.

Hope resisted the urge to scream; the silence was overpowering, and she could almost hear her own organs working. It was a nauseating sensation, and she rubbed her arms, cursing Jhansi and all the Pandorans anew. If this was to be her fate, the council could not have thought of a worse one, and Hope fought down the nausea. The placed looked like a ghost town, old signage from a bygone era still clinging to the tiles despite looking like they'd seen better days, and litter covered the platforms and tracks. Only a handful of lights illuminated the darkness, and Hope ran from patch to patch, fearful of what might be awaiting her in the shadows.

She eventually came to a flight of stairs leading up, and she made her nervous way upstairs, until she came to a wooden door. She pushed cautiously on the door, and it opened with a great creaking and squealing of rusted hinges that grated painfully on her nerves. The sight beyond the door was no more heartening; a deserted ticket hall stretched in either direction as far as the eye could see, as dirty and dingy as the platforms, and just as dimly lit. Hope stepped out, rubbing her arms again, jumping as the door slammed shut behind her, seemingly unaided, the echoes chasing each other up and down the cavernous space for what seemed a very long time afterwards, setting bats to screeching and fluttering. Hope covered her head with her arms as they flew past, the drafts raised by their wings buffeting, but eventually, they settled, and Hope cautiously lowered her arms, heart pounding. Nothing in this vast, dark hall told her of a way out, so she turned right and made her nervous way across the dusty floor, biting her lip as small

things

skittered away from her questing feet. Bats sometimes squeaked from the ceiling, but no more panicked flights came, much to her relief. Her nerves, though, jangled unmercifully every time something small skittered away from her, and by the time she reached another set of doors at the far end of the hall, she felt herself only moments away from madness.

This is hell,

she told herself.

Maybe Pandora and all its horrors was just a dream. Maybe I did drown in that river, and I imagined all of it, and now I've "come back to life" in this place.

It certainly felt like hell, and Hope bit her lip hard. She didn't want to face whatever was outside, but neither did she want to stay in this deserted station with its echoes, its bats, and other unnamed things. And

surely

someone had to be out there, someone who could tell her just what the blazes was going on. It had to be better than in here, Hope told herself.

Anything

had to be better than the silent horrors she'd endured ever since she'd stepped off the train.

Chapter 25

Hope stepped out into a ghost town, and she felt renewed nausea at the sight. Empty buildings lay crumbling around her under a bleak grey sky, and she felt more like throwing up than ever. There was a washed out, dingy cast to the air, as if the place had been frozen in time, only for time to catch up and obliterate everything she saw around her. A bitter, metallic taste coated her tongue as she stood there, and she very nearly threw up on the spot. It took all she had to fight the urge, and by the time she recovered her spinning senses, she became aware of the eyes. There were no people, but she felt the eyes on her all the same, and she shrank against the closed doors of the station. She suddenly felt that being in there would be safer than being out here, but when she pushed the doors, they wouldn't budge, and she cowered, realising she was trapped, with no way to go but forward.

She didn't dare enter any of the crumbling buildings, fearful she might be locked in there with no way out, but as she made her way through the silent streets, she could feel the eyes on her more strongly than ever. Sometimes the sensation was so powerful she spun, fearing what she might see. But nothing met her terrified eyes, and she always went on with fear gnawing at her heart after every encounter. She had no way of telling what the time was, but time didn't matter in this silent place full of ghosts, and Hope felt more and more like an interloper, wishing she could turn back the clock and let Jhansi take her to the station, rather than acting like a loon and getting herself sent to this place.

"Hello."

Hope screamed, clutching her heart as she spied a little girl in a red dress standing before her, holding a red balloon in one tiny hand. "You scared the life out of me!" Hope exclaimed, heart hammering. Her next words died in her throat, however, when she realised the girl was gone, and renewed fear crept its way down her spine. She shivered, rubbing her arms as she looked around, wondering if the solitude was driving her mad.

"Hello."

Biting back her scream, Hope turned, and there was the little girl again, holding her balloon. But the balloon and the dress were blue this time, and Hope rubbed her eyes. Once more, an empty street met her gaze, and she felt a terror greater than any she'd known up to that point. Either she was going crazy, or there

was

a little girl here.

"Hello."

The little girl was now wearing green, with a green balloon.

"Hello."

Yellow dress, yellow balloon.

"Hello."

Purple dress, purple balloon.

"Hello."

Now there were

hundreds

of little girls, wearing dresses and carrying balloons in all the colours of the rainbow. And as Hope stared in mounting horror, none of them vanished. They came on in silence, smiling, their eyes black and dead and empty, and Hope screamed, trying to find a way through the ever-growing crowd of little girls. But they were thick as ants on abandoned food, and they spoke again, their voices merging into a cacophony of distorted sound as their one word greeting filled the air.

"Hello. Hello. Hello."

Hope screamed, covering her ears, bracing herself for horror as the girls came ever closer to her. But just as the first questing hand reached out, the girls vanished, and Hope blinked, tense as she surveyed the street. She waited, eyes wide and staring, but no girl - or legion of girls - reappeared. It took her a very long time to muster the courage to start walking again, but as she took that first step, the staring eyes vanished, and Hope let out a small breath of relief. Whatever horror had been conjured up, it had clearly been a test, to either frighten her or prove some hidden facet in her character. Either way, she felt very wrung out as she resumed her nervous trek across the city, and she prayed that any further "tests" wouldn't be as nerve-wracking. She knew she wouldn't be able to stand up to another horror such as the one she'd just been forced to endure.

Chapter 26

As night began to fall, Hope began seeking shelter. She was footsore, hungry, and in desperate need of a toilet, but she feared there'd be no resources of which she could partake. She feared being on the streets after dark even more, however, and, finally, she found an abandoned swimming pool. Leaves and other debris littered the tiled bottom, and the place as a whole was in a dreadful state of disrepair. Bats chittered as she stepped inside and she stiffened, her heart hammering. But they soon died down, and she let out a sigh of relief as she picked her way across the floor, holding her breath lest she waken more apparitions like the one that had accosted her in the street.

Between one step and another, the scenery changed, and Hope's eyes widened as she saw the pool come to life. Families played and swam in the crystalline waters, while swimmers did laps, or dived from the board at the deep end. Lifeguards kept a watchful eye on the scene, making sure no one was in distress, and Hope's hand went to her heart. When two children walked right through her, she bit down a scream of terror, but then the people fled, and she beheld the pool as it was; empty, derelict, and dirty.

Hope swallowed. This was worse than the legion of little girls outside, and for a moment, she preferred them to the eerie scene she'd just witnessed. But then she recalled how they'd almost stolen the life from her with their greedy hands, and she decided she was much better off in here. But first, she had to find a toilet, and pray that it was in working order. She doubted that was the case, but something had to be better than nothing.

Miraculously, she did find a toilet, and even more surprising, it was clean and flushed properly. Hope washed her hands in record time, however, fearing that this was another illusion, solid as everything felt, and she hurried back out to the pool. It remained as deserted as it had when she'd first walked in, but she didn't dare try and curl up in the shallow end to get some sleep, lest she find herself underwater and drowning. Then again, she told herself, since the illusion she'd seen before

had

been just an illusion, she probably wouldn't drown if she chanced to go into another vision, since it wouldn't affect her any more than the children running through her had.

Even so, she gingerly stepped down into the shallow end, holding her breath just in case. When nothing happened, she sat, resting her back against the chill marble. At least down here, she was a bit more sheltered, but even so, she didn't feel ready to lower her guard for a moment. There was no telling what

might happen if she closed her eyes, even for a few seconds. But the need for sleep overrode the need for caution, and soon, Hope's eyes grew heavy, and her head started to nod despite her best efforts to keep awake. Sleep won, however, and her last thought was a desperate prayer that she might wake up on Pandora - that all that had happened to her today had been no more than a horrible nightmare.

Chapter 27

After several hours, Hope woke, and her eyes widened when she saw she was deep underwater, and she clapped a hand over her mouth in horror when she realised this was no illusion - she was deep underwater, and she was almost out of air. Kicking with all her strength, she managed to break the surface, gasping once her head was above water. But she had no chance to recover; something seized her foot and pulled her back under, away from the life-giving air. No matter how she kicked and flailed, the force holding her was too strong; already the precious air she'd managed to garner was running out, and she was being pulled deeper and deeper.

But then the force holding her let go, and she kicked desperately, lungs burning as she ran out of air, fearing she might not make it this time. She managed to break the surface with only seconds to spare, and her eyes widened when she saw she was bone dry, still sat in the shallow end of the pool where she'd taken refuge earlier in the evening. The moon shone pale and cold through the broken windows, dappling everything in dense white light and deep shade.

Hope swallowed, her heart still racing from the nightmare from which she'd just woken. Or had it been real? She could no longer tell what was real and what wasn't, and as she climbed out of the pool, she knew she had to do something before she lost what was left of her mind. But when she made her way to the doors, she found them sealed shut, even though they'd been lying on the ground when she'd first come here several hours ago. It seemed she had to go on, and she turned back to the pool, her heart hammering again. Nothing in her nightmare clued her as to how to go on, but she knew that, somewhere, there was a way out of this place. She just had to take a deep breath and take the plunge.

Stepping into the pool again, she sat down, closed her eyes, and took a deep breath...

...and she was underwater again, swimming for the bottom. Somewhere there was a way out, and she prayed she'd have the air to get to whereever she was going. But it was wholly dark, and no lights showed her the way. To make matters worse, she was already running out of air, and she felt her way along the bottom, heart pounding loudly, lungs burning as the air ran out.

Then her questing fingers found something. An entrance! She pulled herself along until she felt the portal which would take her on, and she pulled herself through, squeezing through the painfully tight passage. It seemed to go on forever, but just as she thought she might drown, she felt the space around her open up, and she kicked upwards, breaking the surface with a gasp. The passage had widened enough to let her stand up, and she stood shivering in the waist deep water, teeth chattering in the cold air. And though she hadn't heard anything, she knew the passage behind her was now closed. But as she started wading through the water, she didn't care. She'd left the creepy city behind with its ghosts and its bats. Wherever she was headed had to be better than the horrible place she'd left behind. And when she got to where she was going, she'd make sure Jhansi and all her miserable countrymen

paid

for the hell they'd put her through, starting from the moment they'd forced her to leave her daughter behind, to the terrifying moment her train had emerged in the dead city. And they were going to pay

big,

Hope promised.

Chapter 28

The tunnel eventually opened out into a cavern larger than anything Hope had ever seen in her life, lit from end to end with hundreds of torches, turning the place into a grotto fit for a fairy king or queen. But Hope's pleasure in the sight was shattered when she saw Jhansi standing on the ledge near where the tunnel let out, and with a snarl of incoherent rage, Hope clambered out of the water and threw herself at the Pandoran woman with intent to kill her with her bare hands. Jhansi, however, proved herself slicker than a snake; in short order, Hope found herself on the ground, and she spat out dirt and blood as she tried to get up, only to find Jhansi's foot planted firmly in her back. "Haven't you humiliated me enough?" Hope demanded. "It's not enough you put me on a train to hell, but then you show up just when I thought I was free of you! What the hell is going on?"

"I had to do this," Jhansi said, her voice tight with anger. "If you hadn't acted up in Isonor, I wouldn't have been forced to send you on a different train. But I had no choice!"

Hope almost laughed. "You had no choice," she said. "My God. They really taught you how to lie in that police academy, didn't they? You knew full well where you were sending me, and the moment I get full use of my hands, I'll beat you to a bloody pulp!"

"Shut

up!

" Jhansi snapped, seizing her by the hair and hauling her to her feet. Her pupils were dilated to the point her irises couldn't be seen, and had she a tail, it'd be fluffed out to twice its size. "You have no

idea

what you're doing," the policewoman said. "I

have

to do this - otherwise I'll get my fur handed to me on a silver plate, without so much as a chance to say goodbye to my daughter!"

"What the hell are you talking about?" Hope demanded, rubbing her skull and cursing the Pandoran woman's strength. "You won't

tell

me what's going on, so how the hell do you expect me to act? I'm supposed to go meekly along like a lamb to the slaughter? Is that what you did to Saanvi's mother? To all the other mothers who supposedly 'miscarried' their children, only to be drugged and induced into early labor?"

Jhansi took a deep breath. "If I don't do this the right way," she said through gritted teeth, "you

and

I,

and

the women you're so carelessly endagering, are all going to

die,

very slowly, and

very

painfully. I'm doing this the way I've been taught, and your loud mouth is risking our skins almost as much as if I'd brought you here directly!"

"You don't expect me to trust you, not with the way you've been treating me ever since you hauled me off to the lockup," Hope pointed out. "If you don't at least give me some sort of hint, I'll go back into the pool and find my own way back."

"You can't," Jhansi said, sounding almost apologetic. "You may have worked it out already, but if you go back into the water, you'll drown. The moment you came out was the moment the defences came back up; if you go back in, you'll be at the mercy of the creatures who live on the bottom, and they are

not

kind. They'll drag you down, and likely devour you while you're still drowning. Not a pleasant way to go, and I'm sure you don't want to find out what happens when you piss off the people into whose care you've been thrust, whether you like it or not."

"There you go, spinning more crap," Hope said, folding her arms. "Look, just tell me straight; are we about to walk into another abandoned city? Or are we going back to Isonor where I'll be subject to yet another stint in jail before you put me on the

correct

train back to Earth?"

"No and no," Jhansi said. "And that's all I'm telling you, unless you can promise me you'll grow the fuck up and actually

listen

to what I'm saying!"

Hope rolled her eyes. "Let's just get this farce over with," she said crossly. "I really don't give two shits anymore."

Jhansi sighed. "I wish I could tell you more," she said, sounding regretful for the first time since the whole jail incident. "But if I did, I'd be in more trouble than you could ever imagine, not just from the guardians of this place, but from the people back home. Right now, there's not a lot keeping them from being able to get into my head; if I say the wrong thing, they

will

get in, and then we're

all

dead, do you understand me?"

"No," Hope said bluntly. "But I suppose it's going to have to do for now."

"Then follow me, and keep your damn mouth shut," Jhansi told her curtly. "If you dare speak until I say you can, I'll throw you in the pool myself and take

great

comfort out of getting rid of an insolent

child

who hasn't the sense to keep her big mouth

shut!

"

This seemed like bait, but Hope wasn't going to rise to it, and she fell in behind Jhansi, wondering what sort of fresh hell awaited her. She no longer hoped it would be better than the ghost city she'd left behind; in fact, she felt the ghost city and all its horrors would be

far

preferable to what waited for her on the other side of the cavern.

Chapter 29

What stood on the other side of the cavern was not a fresh hell, but instead a wonderland beyond anything Hope could ever have dreamed, and her eyes widened when she saw the pegasus standing before them, its wingspan a magnificent sight to behold. Her jaw dropped in wonder, but, obedient to Jhansi's instructions, she kept her mouth very firmly shut. The pegasus reminded her of the creature she'd seen in the council hall on Pandora, but compared to the gorgeous animal she saw before her, the pegasus she'd seen prior was only a crude copy, a pitiful attempt at capturing the sheer beauty and grace of the creature standing before her.

The pegasus bent its head as the two women approached. 'You see now how my brethren have been enslaved,' the creature said, its voice a deep bass in Hope's mind. 'They have been bred to be lesser, and they live out their days in slavery to the whims of the corrupt council.'

Hope glanced nervously at Jhansi, who gave her a curt nod. "They're... definitely not the same as you," the girl said. "I'm sorry, but seeing you... the pegasus I saw on Pandora looks like a child's drawing."

'You speak truth,' the pegasus told her. 'And you will have seen the other creatures there as well, all of whom have been bred in the same way. As the elves have also been enslaved and bred. They have no more power in that council than does a fly in the presence of a frog.'

"Then it's the Pandorans who have the real power," Hope said, horrified.

"Now you see why I didn't want to say anything," Jhansi told her. "If I said something, they'd catch on and have me arrested the moment they got their hands on me. Queen Tanila's power only extends so far, and her protection only lasts so long as I keep my mouth shut and don't say anything. That's why I had to be so cagey with you, and I'm sorry. I know it's going to take you a good long while to trust me again, but it had to be this way. We're safe now, so yes, the Pandorans are the ones running the show, and yes, everything you said in the cave and on Pandora is true."

Hope shivered and rubbed her arms. "Give me time," she told Jhansi. "I can't trust you yet, but at least you've told me that my fears are warranted. What

is

going to happen to my daughter, and to the other babies thought dead at birth?"

"That's a longer story," Jhansi told her. "Queen Tanila will tell you all, but you're going to be better off hearing it from the horse's mouth, so to speak. No offence, Lathon," she said to the pegasus.

'None taken,' he assured her, speaking in both women's minds now. 'But yes, as Chika said, you're better off hearing the truth about your foals from the women who suffered the most at the hands of those you call Pandorans."

Hope looked at Jhansi - Chika, rather - and saw for the first time that the other woman's skin was now pale golden fur. And she

did

have a tail, which was presently lashing in quite an agitated fashion, while the ears poking up through her hair were half-laid back. Things, Hope realised, had gotten a

hell

of a lot more confusing. But as the two women and the pegasus began making their way across the meadow towards the gleaming city in the distance, Hope took comfort in knowing that soon, some of the mystery surrounding the Pandorans' obsession with her child - and other babies - would be solved. She just prayed it wouldn't be too late for her daughter, or for the son taken from Emily and misrepresented as dead.

Chapter 30

As they drew closer to the city, Hope saw that Isonor had copied the design - down to every last detail. But as with Lathon, the elven city far surpassed Isonor, as did the elves who went about the visitors on their daily business. And unlike the strict breeding Hope recalled from her one meeting with the five elven chiefs, the elves were all of different hair and eye colours, making them one race instead of five separate tribes. Hope didn't need to ask to know that it had been from stolen children from which the five tribes had been bred back on Pandora, and her heart ached as she realised for the first time that her loss was minimal compared to the losses these beautiful people had suffered so long ago. But she knew the elves were doing all they could to protect those first human women who'd suffered, regardless of the desire of the Pandorans to take them back.

Queen Tanila met them in the beautiful throne room, a tall woman with blue-black hair and green eyes. Her age was hard to determine, but she had the eyes of one who had seen much, yet she still retained an air of being in the present, and Hope felt like she could trust this tall, regal woman with anything. "You are not the first to suffer at the whims of the Pandorans," the queen told her, as the three women sat on stools before the throne, cups of tea at their elbows and sweet cakes on a little tray in between the stools. "The first group of Earthen women suffered the same; if their babies were not taken early from their bodies, they were taken away at birth, and not one of the women could raise protest, lest they be imprisoned until they died of old age. Not that the Pandorans would let them go in any case; they knew too much."

"I was an accomplice against my will," Chika confided, glaring at her tea as if imagining a Pandoran was in her grip. "Saanvi was given to me with strict orders that I raise her as my own and never tell her of her true origins. I asked them what had happened to her mother, but I was threatened with my people's extermination if I didn't keep my mouth shut. So I went along with it, but I dug very quietly and subtly, and soon I found out that Saanvi's mother had been told her daughter had died during birth. I didn't get very far; the police nabbed me and threatened me again if I didn't cease my enquiries. To make me even more compliant, they forced me to link my mind to the council, who've used that link ever since to make sure I did as I was told.

"But I wasn't going to be muzzled; I applied to the police force so I could be in a better position to help Saanvi's mother and the other Earth women who'd had their babies taken from them. Over time, I earned the council's trust, and they relaxed their vigil. But the link was never dissolved, and I had to watch my step at every turn. I worked my way up through the ranks, until I reached lieutenant, and from there, I used my powers to inquire very carefully into the fate of the first group of women. They were still in Isonor, but they were forbidden from leaving, treated like queens by their husbands so they were lulled into a false sense of belonging. But they were never given citizenship, and they were not permitted to return home to Earth, lest they tell tales. Not that anyone would've believed them, as you well know."

"That's why Emily and Mia aren't allowed to leave," Hope guessed. "They're being treated like queens, but in reality, they're prisoners."

Chika nodded. "It all came to a head the day you were made to leave your daughter behind," she said. "At that point, the council realised I'd been digging, and, furthermore, that I'd been in contact with Queen Tanila. She reached out to me when I stumbled into her realm by accident around five years ago, and she told me that it had been no accident; I'd been guided to her realm on purpose, and she told me she could save the first group of Earth women. So we worked together to get them shipped out to Felalnor, and they've been living here ever since. But the council didn't like that very much when the truth came out, and they came down on me like a ton of bricks. I had to disavow any knowledge I had of the truth, but they've been keeping me on a very tight leash ever since. That's why I had to be so harsh with you; Queen Tanila's power is not foolproof, and if the council ever broke through her protection spell, it'd all be over, and I'd be dead the moment they got their hands on me. And they wouldn't hesitate to come to Felalnor in a full-scale invasion either."

"I guard this realm with my life," Tanila said. "But I cannot force people to do my bidding. That is the way of the Pandorans, and I will not stoop to that level. Yet, if they ever did come here, they'd find an unpleasant welcome waiting for them. I cannot stop them, but nor will I make it easy for them."

"The ghost city," Hope guessed. "I managed to get through it relatively unscathed, but if the Pandorans came through, they'd have a much harder time."

"A truly difficult time awaits any who come here via that route with ill intent in their hearts," Tanila agreed. "Its sorrowful history contains a fearsome power that has been warped over the decades since the incident which caused it to fall into its current state of disrepair. Any going through with truly malicious intent will suffer a hundredfold the trials you endured, child."

"I'm so sorry about that," Chika added, looking genuinely remorseful. "But the council were getting very close to realsing I'd lied to them, and I had to send you to Felalnor the long way around to throw them off my scent. Unfortunately, I could feel the probes getting stronger the day I met you outside the hospital, and locking you away was only a stopgap measure that hasn't really done much for protecting us both. I had to appeal to Queen Tanila to bring me here directly, which was why I was waiting for you when you came through the portal. And I wasn't lying about the guardians in the water; they're not nice, and had you tried to escape, you would've died just as messily as I described."

"You're forgiven for that," Hope told her. "I'm still rattled by it all, so if I'm a bit cautious around you for a little while, I'm sorry."

"No offence taken," Chika said with a wry grin. "I'd have a hard time trusting me either."

Tanila smiled as she rose. "Now it is time for you to meet your predecessors," she told Hope. "You will see one individual who you feel has deceived you, but please, be a little gentler with him than you were with Chika - for which no one blames you, I might add. But he has been as blameless in this matter as Chika has, and I would not have your first meeting get off to a bad start."

Hope blinked, then nodded. If Eldon had been working behind the scenes as tirelessly as Chika, then he'd be just as innocent. Still, as the queen led them deep into the palace, she vowed to keep her guard up just a little bit. She had no real reason to doubt Chika now, and she certainly didn't doubt the queen. But things had gone to hell in a handbasket too much for Hope to feel entirely relaxed, and though she hated herself for it, she knew no one blamed her. It was, she reminded herself, an entirely normal reaction after the hell through which she'd been ever since being forced to leave her daughter behind.

Chapter 31

The small party eventually made their way out into a garden, the likes of which Hope had never seen before, and her eyes were wide as she followed the queen, with Chika and Lathon behind her. It reminded her of Eldon's garden back on Pandora, and when they rounded a corner, there he was, seated on the edge of a fountain, running his fingers disconsolately through the water. He looked as if he'd aged twenty years since the last time Hope had seen him, shortly before her marriage to Arjun, and her heart went out to him. "Did he get caught?" she whispered to Chika.

The feline woman nodded. "Well, he was on the verge of getting caught," she whispered back. "Like me, he's been working tirelessly behind the scenes to try and stop the council's plan, and they were very close to realising the two of us were working in concert to defy their rule. He had to go on the run to avoid being caught, and he's a marked man now, with a price on his head that would make your eyes water."

Hope shivered. Suddenly, she didn't feel like she wanted to know just what

was going on, but then Eldon looked up and saw them, and it was his turn for his eyes to go wide when he saw Hope. "Love?" he said, taking a hesitant step forward. "My God, I thought ..." He stopped and managed a lopsided grin. "I'm guessing your timely arrival means Chika got to you in time."

Hope smiled, but her heart broke when she saw, despite his joy, how sad he still looked, and she gave his hands a squeeze. "She did, though she was a bit, ah, rough about it."

Chika snorted. "You mean I was a right bitch to you, and I deserve to be called every name under the sun," she said. "I've already explained my part," she added to Eldon. "I think it's all been a bit much, so go easy on her."

"I've had to 'go easy' all my life," Eldon muttered, but he kept a tight grip on Hope's hand as they found places to sit. "Chika's already filled you in," he said to Hope, "so I'll gloss over the gritty details and get to the point. In case you were wondering about that lovely little display I put on when you all arrived in Isonor, I had very good reason. Aoife, Emma and Daisy were all spies for the council. They'd been sent to Earth because the higher ups had got wind I wasn't all I appeared on the surface. I recognised them immediately, and I had to act very fast to throw them off the scent. Emma and Daisy, as you know, no longer have memories of Pandora, and they believe themselves to be ordinary Earth women, and Aoife crossed the Wheel and was thus no longer a threat."

"Good God," Hope murmured, horrified. "So why was Aoife so hell bent on removing me back to Earth?"

"She knew you weren't entirely sure about the venture," Eldon told her. "And she felt I had 'too much influence' on you. She wanted to separate you from the others so she could question you in more detail, but it failed, because Chika got a tip off, and was able to turn the train around before it could make it through the portal to Earth. And she wanted to get her hands on your daughter by any means necessary, even if it meant... well, I won't say it."

Hope had gone sheet white by this point, and she shook her head. "No need," she said in a tight voice. "Thank God she failed! But this all means the council knew, or were getting close to knowing, that you and Chika were playing them false."

"Yup," Eldon said grimly. "I tried finding you after you went into hospital, but no one was saying anything, so I alerted Chika to the fact things had gone very badly wrong, and high-tailed it out of here a day or so ahead of the arrest warrant sent out after me. I can't ever return to Pandora, and good riddance to the place! But this leaves your daughter and Emily's son in grave danger. I honestly believe they'd rather see the two of them dead than reunited with their mothers."

"We have to stop them," Hope insisted.

"Oh, there's no doubt about that," Eldon agreed, pulling her to her feet. "But first, you need to meet the women who were 'recruited' the first time around, and then you'll get a better idea of just what the hell is going on."

Hope shivered as he led her into the garden, with the others following close behind, renewed fear for her daughter warring with her desire to get to the bottom of the mystery behind Pandora's mysterious lack of women and children. She had a nasty feeling finding out would somehow be worse than knowing.

Chapter 32

The three women to which Eldon brought them were older, and haggard-looking, as if life had robbed them of their most precious treasures. Nevertheless Abigail, Edna and Ruth were courteous in their greetings, and once the requisite pleasantries had been exchanged, Abigail told the story of their encounter on Pandora. "We were recruited, same as you," she told Hope. "We didn't want to believe Dorian, but he painted such a glowing picture of the place that we couldn't help but wonder if he really was telling the truth."

Hope looked at Eldon. "My predecessor," he told her in a low voice. "Very charismatic, and able to charm the birds from the trees with just a word or two."

Abigail gave a bitter smile. "He was very charming," she agreed. "So when the ship arrived to take us to Pandora, we all found ourselves reassessing our view of him. Pandora itself was very welcoming, and the council made us feel right at home. They didn't make us official citizens, but told us we had all the rights and priviledges of citizens, so that we were able to move freely about the city.

"In time, we all fell pregnant, but that was when the 'disease' began making its way through our ranks. At the end, only myself, Edna and Ruth were alive, and we were locked away in our homes so no harm would come to us, so said our husbands. But we were also forbidden contact with anyone not of our households, and we couldn't even talk to one another, lest it bring 'undue distress'. In reality, we were isolated, and when our children were born, they were whisked away. We were told our babies had died, and we were not even permitted to grieve for them. Every time we began to feel sorrow over our lost children, we were rebuked and told to be silent, lest we be locked up forever. We didn't want that, so we buried our grief and tried to live life as best we could. Our husbands couldn't do enough for us, but we felt like we were being given the Pandoran equivalent of hush money so we wouldn't dig too deeply into the fate of our children."

"Chika came to us five years ago," Ruth said, taking up the story. "She told us that our children had

not

died, and that they were being kept somewhere secure so no one but the council could get to them. Chika couldn't tell us just why our children had been taken from us, but she said she could get us off Pandora, but it would be a difficult journey. We didn't want to believe her, because Pandorans had lied to us the whole time we were there, but she assured us she was on our side, and she showed us her true form as you see her now, to further prove she was firmly against the council and their twisted game. So we trusted her, and after one of the most nightmarish journeys I've ever gone through, we came here, and we've been residents of Felalnor ever since, given full freedom to roam the land at will, with no one to tell us what we can and can't do."

"But we're exiles here," Edna said. "We have the run of the place, but we're trapped here, not by our fault, but by the desire of the council. They know we've escaped, and they're desperate to get us back so we can't 'tell tales', even though it's been sixteen years since our children were taken from us. If they got their hands on us again, we'd be imprisoned in the darkest dungeons the city has to over, and likely left to rot until we crumble into dust. It's not a pleasant fate, you can be sure; but despite all that, we are content enough here, even though we do sometimes wish we could return to Earht and leave all this behind." She sighed. "And it got even worse when we found out their 'disease' is deliberately engineered to kill the weak, or the ones more likely to see through the Pandorans' facade of peace."

Hope shivered. "I had a feeling it was something like that," she said slowly. "But if that's the case, why didn't it kill me? Or leave me barren?"

"You were too precious to be risked," Edna said. "You see, your daughter, as well as the son of your friend Emily, are the 'perfect' children the Pandorans have been seeking. That's why countless women have been 'recruited', and why so many women and children have died, because they don't have the genes the Pandorans need. They began their 'disease' as a culling method to weed out less desirable folk, but it's gotten out of their control, which is why they genuinely do have few women of childbearing age left. But they could fine-tune it to some extent, which is why you and your two friends were spared. In any case, they have what they want now, and they can still bring the disease to a halt, which is still within their power. They have two children who, by the most unsual turn of luck, have antigens in their blood which will create so perfect they will supersede any breeding program the Pandorans have attempted before."

"In other words, their endless attempts to breed Earth women to their males, or elven children to human children, have failed miserably," Tanila said, her voice deeply bitter. "Many moons ago, five of my people were stolen, as were a mermaid, a dragon, a centaur, a pegasus, and a unicorn. They were all bred accordingly to species on Pandora, and their descendants have been bred to one another, and to more Pandorans, to try and create their perfect raise. But now they have their seeds, and thus, those two innocent babies will be kept separate from everyone else, allowing them to be raised to believe they are Pandoran. They will be forbidden contact to ensure they will be completely compliant with the council's will, and when the time comes, it is the council's hope they will submit to their destiny without complaint."

"Which brings us to now," Eldon said. "The council have pinpointed their key figures are missing. They shouldn't really care too much about the older ladies - no offence, by the way - but they do care desperately to get myself, Chika, and Hope back under their control. Hope in particular will be highly sought after, because if her firstborn has this antigen, future children will likely have it as well. If they get their hands on her, she'll be kept as a brood mare until she's worn out."

"Over my dead body," Hope snapped, shivering with revulsion at the idea. "But why didn't they try that with you?" she asked the older women.

"We were told that their 'disease' had rendered us barren," Ruth said shortly. She sighed. "I'm sorry. It still stings after all this time. But that's what they told us; we were barren, and could no longer conceive. Well, joke's on them; we had tests done on us when we arrived here, and we've somewhat aged backwards to ensure we're still able to carry and bear children. Not that we're too keen on the idea, but it would be nice to have a few young ones running around to help take some of the old pain away."

Hope nodded her understanding. "We've got to stop them somehow," she said.

"How?" Chika asked.

"I don't know," Hope admitted. "But if we put our heads together, we might be able to come up with a way to get the babies back without spilling a drop of blood."

"They won't give the tykes up that easily," Eldon warned. "They'd prefer to kill them rather than see them with their rightful mothers."

Hope sighed. "I'm not giving up without at least

trying to find a solution that doesn't involve us banging our heads against a brick wall!" she said angrily. Before anyone could say anything, she got up and stormed off, swearing as the tears streamed down her cheeks for a very long time.

Chapter 33

Hope wasn't sure for how long she wandered, or how far, but eventually, she stepped into a grove with a peaceful pond shimmering under the light of lanterns in the trees nearby. She stopped, wiping fresh tears from her eyes, finally calming down from her burst of emotion. She hadn't meant to explode, but frustration had got the better of her, and she perched herself on a gnarled branch that arched over the water, the peace calming her jangled nerves.

She knew the others were right. Getting the two babies back would be near impossible without a solid plan, and the council would simply remove the children, or execute them outright, rather than have them freed by their parents. And Queen Tanila's realm was already on the verge of being invaded by the Pandorans, if what Chika and Eldon said was true. The haunted city would do for a majority of the invaders, and the guardians in the lake would finish off the rest. But that still left the infants' fate in the balance, and Hope sighed.

"Hello."

Her heart in her mouth, she turned, but instead of the creepy girl she'd seen in the deserted city, she saw a child dressed in purest white, her long golden hair done up in an elabourate ponytail, white flowers entwined in the long locks. Hope quickly revised her assessment; this wasn't a child, but a woman, albeit no taller than the little girl. And then her eyes widened; this

was

the little girl she'd seen!

The woman smiled. "I apologise for the fright I gave you," she said. "But it is my duty to screen all who first arrive in the city. I am the first line of defence, and given the current situation, all my power will be needed to halt the invaders in their tracks."

Hope relaxed. "You're forgiven," she told the woman. "You did scare the life out of me, though. How do you manage to be so, well, creepy when you're definitely

not?

"

"I will tell you all," the woman promised. "But first, I think a cup of tea and some cake will calm you down. I can sense your troubles are still plaguing you."

"Oh, you don't know the half of it," Hope said, as she hopped down and took the woman's proffered hand.

The woman - who was in fact a pixie named Jorel - made Hope feel right at home, despite the fact Hope did feel a little oversized in the small cottage. In the end, she had to sit on the floor, which Jorel didn't mind in the slightest, and after an hour spent talking over tea and some very delightful cake, Hope felt a lot better. "I shouldn't have stormed off like that," she admitted. "But I just don't know what to do.

I know we can't go in there hammer and tongs, but I can't just sit around doing nothing while two innocent babies are subjected to God only knows what

sort of torment the Pandoran council has in store for them."

"I understand your frustrations," Jorel told her. "But your friends are right. The safety of the two babies is paramount, and as you say, you cannot go in there like a bull in heat. It will only cause you to fall back into the Pandorans' hands, or it will have the equally unpleasant outcome of your daughter and Emily's son being either removed or killed."

Hope sighed, but she was no longer as frustrated as she'd been when she'd left the meeting with Queen Tanila. "What is there to do, then?" she asked.

"For now, there is nothing you can do," Jorel said, firmly but compassionately. "I can feel the desire to do something burn in you like a fire, and I know better than anyone how much it galls to have to sit and smother that fire. But letting it blaze out will cause more harm. For now, you and your friends will have to abide here. The three of you are criminals in the

Pandorans' eyes; Chika and Eldon stand to be executed, and you will be imprisoned, watched night and day, and forced to breed more so-called 'gifted' children."

"No thank you," Hope said crossly. She sighed again. "But you're right. And we've already got war on the doorstep as it is-- What's wrong?" she demanded, as Jorel's eyes turned black. But she already knew what had happened, and she forced herself to put her empty teacup on the floor before she accidentally smashed it. Time seemed to stop, until, after what felt like an eternity, Jorel's eyes returned to their cornflower blue colour, and her face was sheet white.

"A man called Arjun approaches," she said, her voice strained. "He comes with a man called Jaiden, and they are beyond angry."

Hope rose, the blood draining from her face. "I have to get back," she said urgently.

Jorel nodded. "I cannot escort you back to the queen," she said, "but you have only to retrace your steps. You will not get lost, but you must not tarry. I have to invoke powers that will strip the soul from your body if you linger too long, and I would not bring injury to a friend."

Hope needed no further urging; after a quick goodbye, she left the treehouse and hit the ground running. She couldn't remember exactly which way she'd come to reach Jorel's house in the first place, but she did remember some of the landmarks she'd passed by, all on her left. She just had to pass those same landmarks on her right, and she'd be back in the palace gardens. But even as she started her hasty journey back, a horrible sense of doom eclipsed her thoughts, and she knew without being told that Jaiden would easily be able to counter anything Jorel would throw at him and Arjun. She could only pray the guardians in the cavern would make short work of the two invaders before they could spread the word of how to reach the elven city. If even the guardians failed ... she shut that thought off. There'd be time enough to dwell on that when she was back with her friends.

Chapter 34

C hika met her as she came hurrying into the palace gardens. "You look like you've seen a ghost," the feline woman said, gripping her hands tightly. "What's happened?"

Hope took a deep breath. "I met a pixie in the forest," she said, before going into detail about Jorel's powers. When she finished up, Chika had gone sheet white under her fur, and her ears went back as she hissed.

"I

knew

it wouldn't take those two long," she snapped, grabbing Hope's hand and half dragging her along the path. "I can't say I'm surprised that Jaiden came along; he's got the most pull, and he's got the sun elves firmly under his control. I won't go into the uncomfortable details, but you know enough to know he's pushing for two of their children to become part of the new 'breeding program'."

"Bloody hell," Hope groaned. "I'd forgotten all about that, to be honest."

Chika gave her a half-smile as they hurried into the palace. "Hopefully the guardians in the lake will deal with them so we don't have to."

Hope prayed for the same. But she had the nasty feeling that wouldn't be the case; Jaiden would not let himself be stopped so easily, and if her guess was right, he had enough elven magic in him to counter Queen Tanila's, with both hands tied behind his back!

The queen was very pale when the two women came running into her drawing room. Hope's heart sank; being an elf, Tanila would know if her distant kin was using magic to counter hers, and it showed on her face. "He is very strong," she said, her eyes like chips of ice as she called for servants to bring food and drink for the women. As the servants got to work, the queen continued. "But though I am forbidden to take him on directly, it does not mean he is going to get an easy audience."

"He can go fffff-fog himself," Hope said, hastily swapping that word out for the one she'd been about to use.

Tanila gave her a tight smile. "He most certainly can," she said. "If he and his repulsive son manage to get past The Weeds, well, then we shall have to deal with them face to face."

Hope groaned again. "Of course Arjun is his blo- blasted son," she said. "Why am I not surprised?"

"Then you will know he has altered your daughter's DNA so he can be her father in blood as well as legal fact," Tanila said, her eyes compassionate despite the ice.

"I didn't know that, but that doesn't surprise me either," Hope said crossly. "Is there no level to which the man won't stoop?"

She got her answer when Lathon came to the door. 'They have reached the meadow,' he said, his voice as close to open anger as Hope had ever heard from him so far. 'Your orders?'

"They are to be met with a strong guard," Tanila said. "Have two Faceless go with them."

Lathon left in a clatter of hooves, and the queen explained her orders once he'd gone. "The Faceless can nullify all magic, no matter how powerful," she said. "Two will more than suffice to keep Jaiden and his son from using their arts to try and manipulate their way out of the

very

dire trouble they are now in!"

Epilogue

Hope tried telling herself she was safe, but as Jaiden and Arjun were marched in under heavy guard, she couldn't help the shiver that slid down her spine. Jaiden looked as if the whole affair was one massive inconveniece to him, but Arjun gave her a look that spelled trouble, a look that turned to jealous dislike when she tightened her hold on Eldon's hand. He tightened his grip in response, and Hope welcomed the almost bruised sensation; it reminded her she had people in her corner who'd defend her to the very last breath in their bodies.

Arjun, however, was soon caught off guard when he saw Chika in her natural form, and his eyes widened. "You're one of them? " he exclaimed, loathing all over his face.

Chika's ears went back and she hissed. "Yes, I'm one ofthem," she snapped. "You didn't work that out from all your years of spying, you cretin?"

Before Arjun could retaliate, Tanila intervened. "You are a prisoner," she told Arjun in a voice cold enough to cap even the most potent of all active volcanoes. "You have no right to disparage my guests."

"They're fugitives on the run from justice!" Jaiden said angrily, but he wilted when the queen turned her glare on him." You both are prisoners," she said. "From this moment on, you are forbidden to speak unless spoken to."

The Faceless - two silent, black garbed individuals who really did have no faces - never moved. But the prisoners' eyes bulged as they suddenly found their mouths shut, and Hope bit down a giggle in spite of herself. It was rather satisfying to see her former husband and father-in-law brought down a peg or three. Tanila gave her a smile before her expression turned to stone once more.

"You are here by deceit," she told the two Pandorans. "How you managed to win your way past our stringent protections is not a matter to be dealt with right now. What is to be dealt with is the matter of why you came here. Oh, don't look so shocked! You think I am ignorant of what goes on beyond my borders? You truly believe I would not be fully informed as to why Chika and Eldon came seeking my aid five years ago?" She shook her head. "You are truly dimwitted if you think I haven't been actively working with them to undo the tremendous wrong your ancestors visited upon my kind, the wrong which you yet seek to continue with two innocent victims who have no part in your schemes!"

One of the Faceless used their arts to unbind Jaiden's mouth; Arjun blinked, before his eyes went wide. Clearly his ears had been stopped so he couldn't hear what his father was saying, but Hope couldn't find amusement in his outraged expression this time. "We are dying," Jaiden said angrily. "You probably heard a bunch of lies from these two, but I can assure you, it is not as bad as they claim!"

"I subjected them both to truth spells," Tanila said. "They could not lie, even by omission, and every word that came out of their mouths was examined from all angles, until it was determined they were indeed telling the truth about your long-standing campaign to weed out the less 'worthy' of your abused women and children. And I know full well how it's become a monster of its own, a monster of your making."

Jaiden turned a murderous glare on Chika and Eldon - or tried to, at least. Clearly his sight had been blocked as well, and his face contorted in an expression of pure animal rage. "Stop that!" he snapped. "You're not supposed to manipulate things! It goes against your moral code!"

"I am not doing anything," Tanila said simply. "It is your own twisted passions that are working against you. Now, as to your crimes; I cannot do anything about what you and your ancestors have done in the past. Nor can I bring you task for what you are doing now; it is out of my hands, as much as I long to see you and all your kind facing justice. But I can promise you this; you and your son will be returned home.

You will recall all that has happened here, but neither of you will be able to do a thing about it.

If you try, you will find yourselves subjected to the worst nightmares known to humankind. I will not inflict those nightmares on you; they will come from within you. So long as you refrain from declaring war, you will not suffer. But should you even think of attempting an invasion, then those nightmares will torture you, waking and sleeping, until you are jumping at every shadow, until you go insane from lack of sleep for fear of what awaits you in your dreams. And be warned; I am merciful. But my mercy is not to be taken lightly. I could easily go against all I stand for and personally curse the two of you for all eternity. But I choose the higher ground.

That is my mercy; remember it."Jaiden and Arjun - who'd had his ears unstopped during this speech - were both whiter than it was possible for a human to go. Hope didn't blame them; the queen's mercy was a terrible thing to behold, and she clung even closer to Eldon, who put an arm around her and held her tightly."You have no power over us!"Arjun finally managed to get out. "You're bluffing!"

"Try me," Tanila invited. It sounded innocent on the surface, but there was a deep, dark threat under her words. "I invite you to give it your very best go, gentlemen."

She rose. "Escort them to the secret way," she told the Faceless. "Let them see it, for it will do them no good in the long run."

"This isn't over," Arjun warned. He then turned his glare on Hope. "And you haven't gotten off lightly either. You will be brought back to Pandora where you belong, even if you have to be dragged kicking --" He cut off, his eyes widening once more. "What the hell is that?" he demanded, pointing at an empty corner of the room. There was nothing there that Hope could see, but she knew without being told the nightmare geas had taken hold of her former husband already. She wanted to feel sorry for Arjun, but as he and his father were led away, she told herself not to be an idiot. Arjun still had her daughter - his daughter as well, thanks to the DNA manipulation he'd used - under guard. And he planned on mating her against her will when she was older. That cancelled out any soft feeling Hope might otherwise have entertained, and she sighed as she slumped against Eldon, the tension of the meeting draining out of her as reaction set in. As she buried her tears against his shoulder, she thanked God for him and Chika, knowing she wouldn't have been able to handle that nightmare interview without them.

But her tears were also for her daughter, now a helpless prisoner under Pandoran control. There was nothing she or her friends could do, and though Jaiden and Arjun had been rendered powerless, they would double down on their efforts to ensure Hope's daughter would never know she had a mother other than the one to which they would no doubt assign her. And that mother would probably fill her head with all sorts of lies, until Hope was painted as the worst kind of individual possible.

"I wish there was something we could do," she whispered helplessly against Eldon's shoulder. He kissed her hair gently in response.

"There's nothing more we can do, love," he said, helpless rage in his voice as he held her tightly. "But one day, your daughter will learn the truth, and she'll come looking for you on her own, I swear it."

"And I'm still not entirely without resources," Chika added, joining the two of them on the couch. "I can't do much, but I can ensure your daughter is placed with someone who's flown completely under the council radar for almost seventeen years, someone they'd never dream would turn on them."

"Saanvi?" Hope said, startled.

Chika nodded. "Saanvi doesn't agree with the idea any more than I do," she said, "but she's got the good sense to keep her mouth shut and her nose clean. She'll obey the council to the letter, but she'll ensure your daughter is not brainwashed, and if she has to expend some of her own abilities to do so, well, she will."

Hope nodded, feeling better. "Thanks," she said. "And ... I'm sorry."

"There's nothing to be sorry for," Chika told her. "I did you a bad turn, and I've got years to make that up. But I do hope I count as a friend, at least."

"You've never stopped," Hope said, reaching out and giving the feline woman's hand a squeeze. She took a deep breath. "We all might as well get settled down," she told the two cat people (Eldon had chosen to finally shed his own human disguise at that point). "And pray Saanvi can fly under the radar somewhat better than her mother," she added with a small grin. Chika rolled her eyes, but she squeezed Hope's hand tightly, as did Eldon.

"Then I shall declare the three of you citizens in the morning," Tanila said, smiling warmly at them. "It is late, and such matters are better done during daylight hours. For now, I think we all need to rest."

"Good idea," Hope said, yawning as Eldon and Chika helped her to her feet. Matters could definitely be settled in the morning, she told herself. But the most important matter - her daughter - would have to wait just a little bit longer.

And then the Pandorans would really have to watch their step!

www.ingramcontent.com/pod-product-compliance
Lightning Source LLC
Chambersburg PA
CBHW071016180726
48291CB00004B/1483